SIL

ST

OVER 100
GREAT NOVELS
OF
EROTIC DOMINATION

If you like one you will probably like the rest

NEW TITLES EVERY MONTH

If you want to be on our confidential mailing list for our Readers' Club
Magazine (with extracts from past and forthcoming titles) write to:

SILVER MOON READER SERVICES

The Shadowline Building
6 Wembley Street
Gainsborough
DN21 2AJ
United Kingdom
or
sales@babash.com

or telephone
01427 816710
(UK office hours only)

NEW AUTHORS WELCOME

Please send submissions to
Silver Moon Books Ltd.
PO Box 5663
Nottingham
NG3 6PJ
or
editor@babash.com

First published 1998 Silver Moon Books
Second Edition 2004
ISBN 1-897809-57-3

SINFINDER GENERAL

BY

JONATHAN TATE

ALSO BY JONATHAN TATE
A SLAVE FOR THE SINFINDER

1

A woman is not truly conquered until she has been taken like a dog.

Jed and Sam knew that.

Maybe even Lucinda Drake knew it as she ran from them, stumbling through the dense woodland. The snapping of twigs, the thudding of her riding boots against the sodden earth, the grizzled growling of her pursuers, all combined to panic her, so that the noise of her flight was nearly drowned by the sound of her feverish panting.

Her white blouse snagged against a low-hanging branch, the material ripping to expose a frantically bouncing breast—nipple big and pink; hard, like a bullet. Her long blonde hair snagged too, until she tore it free and stumbled onwards. She staggered against a crumbling log and fell headfirst into the damp moss.

From a distance, Jed and Sam saw her tumble. Her body descended and her aristocratic bottom flashed into view.

They stumbled on eagerly, fingers tingling with the need to grope her fleshy buttocks, cocks throbbing with desire for her. The mistress had been promised a fuck in her bottom and a fuck she would get.

Lucinda had squealed and run, horrified at the thought of the crusty old men stripping her buttocks clear of her clothes and taking turns to enter her back-passage with their disgusting cocks.

She'd heard the master—her husband to be—heard him laughing as she'd fled across the fields towards the woodland. She'd heard him urging his two rough farmhands after her, and as she ran, she wished she'd let him have her that morning. John was a cruel man—a man who thought nothing of letting his servants use her.

It was too late for Lucinda now. Her fate was sealed. No amount of pleading would save her from her punishment. Her only chance was to run, and hope against hope that Jed and Sam would give up chasing her. She stumbled through a thicket of brambles, wincing as the sharp thorns scratched her soft skin. There was no chance of them letting her go. No chance at all. They had to catch her, to have her as they had been commanded, if they wanted to keep their jobs.

John wouldn't tolerate failure…

Lucinda tore free of the dense woodland and lurched into a yellow field. Jed and Sam were at her now, like unruly dogs snapping and scratching at her quivering flesh. Jed was behind her, holding her still while Sam ripped away the shredded remains of her blouse and mauled her naked breasts. His fat fingers squeezed the soft white flesh and twisted her big bullet-head nipples.

Lucinda tried to pull away, thrusting her bottom backwards into Jed's stiff groin. "Get off me!" she squealed, and raked the heel of her boot down his shin.

"She's a wild one!" Jed laughed, unperturbed by the sudden pain in his leg. "I'm looking forward to bum-fucking the feisty little bitch and that's a fact!"

Sam tore at her jodhpurs, wrenching them to her knees. Jed dragged her big white pants down, baring her so that her thick pubic bush sprang out towards his accomplice and her round aristocratic buttocks wobbled cheekily, daring Sam to part them and penetrate the tight brownness of her bum-mouth.

"Let go of me!" Lucinda wailed, twisting and turning frantically as she attempted to free herself from their attentions. "I'll have you both soundly flogged for this outrage!" She tried to kick, but the tangled trousers wrapped around her knee-high boots acted as a restraint. "I'll have the skin flogged off your hides!"

Jed and Sam gurgled and laughed again; baring rows of none too white teeth. Sam persisted in his rough massage of Lucinda's succulent breasts. Jed continued to hold her still, with one strong arm wrapped around her stomach, clamping her to him. His other hand folded around the fleshy mound of her left buttock, teasing it away from its mate and opening the deep sweaty cleft that cleaved her cheeks.

"Mistress Drake's all hot and wet from riding that horse of hers this afternoon," he growled, fingers dipping into the clammy crack. His fingertip pressed against the moist ring of anal flesh that throbbed wantonly and Lucinda squealed as the thick digit dug into her.

"I think she's ready for a good hard arse-fuck," Jed declared. He tickled at the rubbery walls of her back-passage, delighting in the resulting whine that emanated from her lips.

Lucinda heard the sound of a zipper, felt Sam press himself into her breasts and take a firm hold of her arms to restrain her, and then felt Jed's hands roughly wrench her buttocks wide apart. Fresh air kissed her anus for a brief second, then she felt the hot, bulbous head of Jed's penis nuzzle against her.

A good hard thrust and Jed was within her, thick cock ploughing forward against the moist walls of her rectum, plugging her up.

"That's nice, Mistress Drake," he whispered. "Now hold nice and still while I give this arse-crack of yours a good hard fucking!"

The farmhand's penis felt like a thick trunk inside Lucinda's bottom, throbbing and hot, stretching her tight brown hole until it was the size of a pink cunt. Jed began to thrust in and out of the mistress's bum; long, firm strokes that sent his sex muscle deep into the darkness of Lucinda's most shameful hole. He admired the brown

7

flesh of her distended anus as he hammered away at her.

Lucinda found herself grasping Sam for support as her bottom was ravaged. She was clamped between the two rugged, ugly men, their breath slaked with the sweet aroma of cider, their hands rough and hard.

"Go on!" Sam urged, clutching her to him, "poke her arse good and hard! Give that tight brown hole a good fuck!"

Lucinda clenched her teeth as the old man thrust himself in and out of her rectum. If only she'd acquiesced with John's wishes; if only she'd let him take her that morning. The constant thrusting and withdrawing of Jed's sex muscle was serving as an excruciating reminder of her foolishness. She was certainly paying a heavy price for her mistake…

"Fuck the shit out of her, Jed!"

…Held upright between the two of them…

"Go on! Harder! Really poke her ringpiece!"

…blouse torn open, jodhpurs and panties twisted at her knees, breasts pressed against the sweat-soaked chest of one assailant, buttocks plied wide and her anus penetrated by the other.

"That's it!" groaned Jed, suddenly digging his fingers into the flesh of her hips, his body stiffening. "Take that, you stuck-up bitch!" Lucinda felt the cock suddenly bulge within her and then its hot fluid was jettisoned into her tripes. The monster slipped from her rectum and, for a second, Lucinda feared something more would follow it.

Then, with fast readjustments, Jed and Sam switched positions.

Lucinda pleaded for mercy as Sam buried his cock to its hilt inside her bottom. Jed held her up now, his hands fondling her breasts, his teeth nibbling at the lobe of her ear. Sam hammered into her anus at a frenetic speed.

His rhythm caused her buttocks to jiggle wildly, the cheeks slapping time and again against his pistoning cock. When he too had pumped his seed into Lucinda, the two men dragged her between them back into the wood. The jodhpurs, twisted at her knees, caused her to stumble, and she dropped to the soft earth.

The old men pulled her up and tugged her trousers back into place. Once in the darkness of the wood, they wrenched them down again and manhandled the semi-naked woman across Jed's legs as he perched himself on a crumbling log.

"Let's see if we can't teach the mistress a lesson in common courtesy!" said Sam.

"Please!" Lucinda whimpered, screwing up her eyes tight as the blood hurried to her head. "What are you going to do to me?" She dug her fingers into the sodden earth. She didn't know why she'd bothered asking the question. She knew what was going to happen; of course she did. There could only be one reason for a woman to be laid out, bottom bare, across a man's knee.

Jed choked a laugh from his throat and confirmed her fears. "We're going to whip your lovely round arse, Mistress Drake!" he exclaimed. "I don't think you'll be so high and mighty after you've had these lovely big bumcheeks of yours tickled with a nice fresh bundle of twigs!"

Sam, who she could see scampering around collecting the twigs, brought what he gathered to his friend. Jed clutched them firmly in his fist, rearranged them to his liking, and then, without the slightest ceremony or warning, brought them down across her naked buttocks.

Lucinda yelped and began to squirm. By the fourth stroke, she was kicking and wriggling uncontrollably.

"She's squeals like one of the master's pigs!" exclaimed Sam, as Jed briskly whipped the mistress's bottom with his bundle of rods. The twigs continued to whistle through the air, each time landing with a crack on the trembling flesh of Lucinda's magnificently round backside. Her bottom cheeks danced wildly as they were whipped, their frenzied contortions occasionally causing her cleft to fold open, flashing her tight brown bum-crack and glistening wet love hole.

"Whip that arse 'til you've flayed the skin off it, Jed," advised Sam as he fondled his own gradually-stirring penis. "That should teach the mistress to be more respectful to the master in future."

Jed striped Lucinda's bottom with the make-shift birch until each of her buttocks burned a fierce scarlet, and the collection of twigs hung limp and useless from his hand; snapped and broken in two. Then he and his companion began to slap away at her naked bottom-flesh with their big rough palms. When they had thoroughly slapped her bottom all over, they held her facedown over the log and parted her cheeks again.

Then they took turns to once more enter her trembling body through the slithery aperture of her anus. Both men erupted within her for a second time, their hot emissions sloshing against the rubbery inner walls of her bumhole...

When they were done with her, Jed and Sam tied Lucinda's wrists together with a thick rope, then hurled its end over the branch of a tree and winched her up until she hung three feet above the mossy ground. They staked the rope to the earth, condemning the mistress to dangle in mid-air. She was to hang there until dusk. And hang there she did, swaying gently from side to side as the branch above her creaked and groaned with the burden of her weight.

As the moon rose and a nearby owl began to hoot its nighttime melody, Lucinda heard the sound of twigs snapping as someone drew near. She moaned softly and twisted around in mid-air. Her muscles ached, her buttocks throbbed, and for all the efforts she had made, she'd been unable to get rid of the leafy carrot the two men had pushed into her anus as a farewell gesture.

"What a pretty picture!" said the master as he approached.

"John!" Lucinda gurgled. "Oh, John! Thank God you're here! Oh John I'm so sorry—I was a bad girl! I know that now!" She was gasping with excitement at her fiancé's arrival, eager for release from the torment of her hanging position.

"I'm glad to hear that," he said casually, and the sound of his cool voice made Lucinda tremble with a heady mixture of anxiety and lust. "I do like the look of this lovely green vegetation sticking out of your bum." He nonchalantly flicked the leaves protruding from her bottom-cleft where a carrot had been inserted. "Jed and Sam did an excellent job."

"Please get me down from here," Lucinda gasped. "I promise to be a good girl in future, really I do!"

Her mind was whirling. She was cold, embarrassed, humiliated and confused—yet she was also strangely aroused.

"We'll take you home now, shall we?" her master suggested, "and you can have a nice long soak in a hot bath."

He removed the stake from the earth and, using his considerable strength to take the weight of her hanging body, carefully lowered her to the ground. "Then we shall see."

Lucinda's gaze burned into him as he set about untying her wrists. "See what?" she asked, a hint of trepidation evident in her voice.

John smiled, his white teeth flashing in the gathering

gloom. "See how well you've learned, of course," he said. "I am not only your husband to be, Lucinda, but also your master, as I am the master of everything and everybody on this estate. I take what I want, because it is mine to take, and I make no exceptions to that rule."

His eyes met hers. There was a steely determination etched into his face which Lucinda had never seen before. "You must learn," he continued, "and learn quickly, my darling—that this beautiful, majestic bottom of yours," his hand squeezed her spanked left buttock, making her wince, "along with the rest of your lovely body, is mine to do with exactly as I please."

He placed a hand on the back of her neck…

"…And that if I wish to fuck it…"

…and gently drew her face towards his, planting a succulent kiss on her mouth…

"…then fuck it is most certainly what I shall do."

John's torch lit the way back through the wood. The couple clambered fences, leapt a narrow stream that trickled down almost apologetically from the hillside looming over the woodland, and eventually found the quiet road leading back to the master's mansion.

Lucinda drew her fiancé's jacket more tightly around her shoulders as they passed the local pub. They could hear wild whoops of laughter emanating from The Birch Twig and Lucinda couldn't help but wonder if Jed and Sam were in there, if maybe they were recounting the story of the afternoon's events to the other locals.

Maybe it was she at whom they were laughing; the high-and-mighty mistress of the manor, who'd been sodomised by two rough farmhands; who'd squealed and kicked while they'd slapped and birched her bum. Maybe they were laughing at the thought of her hanging from a tree branch, tits out, pants at her kneecaps and a carrot stuffed in her bumhole.

She tried to put such thoughts from her mind, and was helped in her attempts by the sudden distraction of car headlights shining brightly in her eyes.

"Visitors," John observed, as he watched the car swing into the small, gravel car park located at the back of the pub. "Now we don't get many of those around here. I hope Bill and Maggie have a nice guest beer on."

Bill supped long and hard from his pint, a moustache of froth forming on his thick upper lip. Old Jack nudged the barman's drinking arm in a good-humoured manner, whooping with delight and then slurping from his own glass as he watched the pub entertainment unfold.

The log fired crackled and spat, its bright red flames coiling upwards like fingers, its heat burning the fronts of Maggie's thighs. Palms of her hands resting against the wall above the fireplace, fingers digging at the crumbling plaster, the flame-haired landlady stood at arms-length from the fire. Her back sloped down at a forty-five degree angle, creating a posture which beautifully presented her hind-quarters to the delighted customers crammed into the bar. Her legs were straight but wide apart, her breasts naked, her big bum thrust outwards.

One of the locals was standing behind and to the side of her. Craggy-faced and impassive, balancing a cigarette between his dry and peeling lips, he was purposefully lashing Maggie's buttocks with a thick leather whip.

"Flay the hide off her, Reg!" came a growled message of encouragement from somewhere within the assembled throng.

"That's the way," piped up another voice, "Whip Maggie's big buns til she says the drinks are on the house!"

The locals roared with approval, all eyes briefly turning towards Bill, casually draped against the bar, guzzling ale.

"How about it, Bill? Drinks all round to save your missus's arse?"

"Bollocks to that!" roared the bull-necked landlord, jovially returning Old Jack's earlier nudge. "You'll not see me handing out free ale just to save her fat cheeks!"

There was another roar, mingling with the clinking of glasses, the sounds of guzzling and the crack of leather on jiggling hide. Maggie was naked except for a pair of nylon tights. Each time the leather bit into her flanks, her breasts bounced like fat melons, swishing from side to side as she squirmed in pain. The lash had done its work, lacerating the nylon so that her punished buttocks were almost entirely bare.

"Another couple of strokes should do it, Bill," urged one of the numerous women who were gathered around, "then we can all have a look at that nice ripe cunt of hers!"

"We can do more than just look!" offered Old Jack, and the resultant laughter thundered around the room until the sound of leather cracking against quivering bum-flesh drew people's attention back to the spectacle.

"Her face is almost as red as her hair!" laughed a young blond man slouched in the corner of the room.

"And her arse!" blurted Old Jack. Again the roars of laughter echoed around the bar.

"Stick your arse right out for the last one, Maggie," urged Reg, taking a final suck on his cigarette before nonchalantly flicking its stub past the big-bottomed redhead into the open fire.

Outside the pub's latticework window, Laura and Sally could hardly believe their eyes. They'd happened to glance into the bar as they made their way from the car park round to the front entrance, and had both stopped dead in their tracks. Now they were crouching down beneath the window ledge, peering in through the slightly-frosted glass and between the various seated and standing bodies, watching the well-endowed Maggie getting her bottom leathered.

"Unbelievable," muttered Laura, "this is just frigging unbelievable!"

"Do you think we should help her?" Sally whispered, "Get the police or something?"

The sudden sound of a twig snapping caused both women to spin around.

"She don't need any help!" growled old Jed, biting down on his pipe.

"But you two ladies," continued Sam, menacingly, "ah well…now that's another matter altogether…"

2

Rough hands clutched at their arms as Laura and Sally were pulled inside the rural Pub. The front door slammed shut, but nobody within as much as batted an eyelid. They were too engrossed in the events unfolding at the bar, for by the time the two girls were manhandled to the doorway, the scene inside the room had changed dramatically.

Maggie was completely naked; the remains of her shredded tights burning on the crackling fire, and was locked in a passionate embrace from her punisher. She was facing away from the audience, her buttocks quivering as Reg's massive hands squeezed and mauled them, roughly massaging the tenderised flesh.

"Get those fat cheeks open, Reggie," encouraged a short, plump woman, hiding behind a pint of yellow cider, "let's have a look at her big fat cunt!"

Reg's fingers crawled into the divide between Maggie's buttocks. He wrenched her hot cheeks apart, opening up the fissure that hid the flesh of her glistening sex. Maggie thrust her bottom backwards to expose herself further, an action that encouraged the plump cider-drinker to demand even more. "Show us her arsehole, Reg—give us a sniff of her ringpiece!" she laughed, and was soon joined in her merriment by her fellow drinkers.

Reg pulled the redhead's bottom cheeks as wide apart as he could, displaying for all to see the tight little opening of her anus, set in a swollen mound of puckered brown flesh.

"How d'you want it, Mags?" chortled her husband from across the bar, toasting his naked wife with a newly-pulled pint of bitter.

"Up her friggin' arse, that's how she wants it!"

whooped the plump cider drinker.

"Nah, ram it in her fat cunt—put her in the pudding club, Reg!"

It was then, as Maggie fumbled with her punisher's trousers, that the arrival of Laura and Sally was noticed. Jed and Sam urged the two struggling girls forward into the main area of the bar.

A sudden hush fell.

Maggie turned towards the new arrivals, her breasts jiggling from side to side as she scraped her long red hair back behind her shoulders.

"And what we got here then?" she asked in a rough, rustic growl.

"We found these two outside, lookin' in through the window," Sam answered, rubbing his nose with the back of his hand.

"Well there's a thing," said the redhead murmured, carefully eyeing the women up and down. "Nosey pair of strangers, are you?"

"We were just looking for a drink," Sally offered tentatively.

"You don't get a drink by looking through the window. All you get yourself is a whole lot of trouble."

"Look, we're sorry," said Laura, hoping an apology might suffice but somehow doubting it. "We didn't mean to interrupt anything and we had no intention of being nosey."

"That's as maybe," it was Bill who spoke, in a low gruff voice, "but you did interrupt and you were nosey."

Laura's eyes flitted from person to person as she tried to gauge the prevailing mood. It was undoubtedly a threatening one. "You've got to admit that this is all pretty weird," she muttered at length. She could feel the words almost choking in her throat as she uttered them. The atmosphere was thick with tension. It was hard for her

17

to keep calm when she was so aware of a dozen or more pairs of eyes boring into her.

"I mean… Sally told me English pubs were pretty unique, but…"

"You never expected to find trouble this side of the pond," Maggie interjected. "Well there's lots of things goes on in the English countryside that most people don't know about." She ran her fingers through her hair, and distractedly began to caress her right nipple. "Problem is, you two do know about this—and that will never do."

Laura tried a faint smile, hoping against hope to disarm the menacing crowd. "So what are you going to do," she questioned, and added as humorously as the situation would allow, "beat us both over the head until we forget?"

Sally instinctively knew that her friend's sarcasm would only serve to incense the redhead. The cold expression etched into the features of Maggie's hard face confirmed the English girl's worst fears.

"Cheeky little bitch, aren't you?" she murmured, raising a menacing eyebrow at Laura. Her gaze flitted towards Sally. "You ought to keep your Yankee friend in check, if you know what's good for you," she warned, "or she'll get you into even more trouble than you're already in." She returned her glare to Laura. "For your information, we don't beat heads here, you little tart," she muttered from between clenched teeth, "we beat arses." She snapped her fingers. "Reg, Frank, clear a couple of tables."

"No!" Sally exclaimed, suddenly realising that her feelings of anxiety were about to take on a more tangible form.

"Jed, Sam, bring those little vixens over here." Rough hands were upon them again, forcing them into the centre of the room. Laura and Sally twisted and turned, making a desperate attempt to break free of their assailants. Two of the more boisterous women in the group stepped forward to assist the farm workers, snatching at the captive girl's hair and tugging at their clothing.

The two friends staggered and stumbled. They squealed as they were pushed forward and sent tumbling into the specially re-positioned tables. Their faces slapped against the wooden tabletops, their breasts pushed against the hard cold surface. A splinter of wood dug into Laura's cheek; Sally gurgled and spat as her face splatted into a puddle of spilt beer.

Strong men weighed down on them, holding them in position, bent over the tables.

"Whip the bitches!" shrieked the cider-drinking woman, "Take the skin off their soft city arses!"

"Get their skirts up, let's have a look at their bums!" cried out Old Jack, who'd staggered across the room towards them, determined to enjoy the forthcoming spectacle. Hands grasped at the two friends' skirts, hitching them up. The two visitors squirmed and wriggled in a futile effort to escape, their frantic contortions delighting the enthusiastic crowd.

"Please God, let us go!" cried Sally, as she felt her lifted skirt flop against her lower back. Almost before the material had settled, hands were at her tights, wrenching them savagely from her waist. Even as she felt the nylon being peeled down her legs, other fingers locked around the waistband of her panties. They, too, were then tugged to half-mast around her knees.

Laura, pressed over the tabletop next to her, was wearing a shorter skirt. The American felt the material being gathered at her hips and then rough fingers snatching at her panties. The tiny garment was peeled down her thighs to the tops of her stockings. Other fingers re-positioned her suspenders, ensuring that every morsel

19

of her bottom was exposed.

From the corner of her eye, Laura saw one of the women in the group reach into her handbag and pull out an implement of some kind, passing it over her head to Sam, who still stood behind her.

"Here," said the woman, "use that on her. That should get her arse smarting nicely!"

Another female voice, somewhere across the room, then said something which left the American in no doubt about what she was going to be beaten with;

"Has anybody got another hairbrush?" she shouted. Her request was followed almost immediately by an outpouring of sobs from Sally. Laura turned her face to look at her friend. Hair and cheek soaked in beer, Sally lay heaving for breath over the table. Her face was contorted into a terrible grimace, her eyes staring wildly. Saliva dribbled from the corner of her mouth as she choked and wailed, fearfully awaiting her spanking.

Laura saw Jed clasp a long-handled brush, passed to him by a woman at the back of the crowd. She heard the words 'paddle their arses, boys!' and gritted her teeth in preparation for the ordeal to come.

Jed and Sam were both wielding hairbrushes now. Laura's view of Jed, standing to the side of Sally's bare bottom, was suddenly obscured by Sam, who repositioned himself in readiness to administer her spanking.

"Alright, lads," growled Bill, "on a count of three, spank their bums!"

"Frigging Hell!" groaned Laura. In spite of her best attempts to wriggle free, she was still firmly in place over the table. She buried her face in her hands and hoped to God Sam would go easy on her ass.

"One…" she clenched her teeth and screwed up her face into a grimace.

"Two…" Sally began sobbing more loudly, the sounds she was making accentuating Laura's own feeling of distress. "Be brave, honey," she murmured, trying to comfort her friend, even as her own ass twitched anxiously.

"Three!"

Laura felt the wooden-backed brush splat against her right buttock, heard the sound of the other hairbrush spank Sally's flesh, and then groaned into the table top as the burning pain coursed through her bottom. She wriggled slightly, but her upper body was held firmly in place.

She hardly had time to recover before a second spank cracked into the flesh of her left bumcheek. "That's the way!" went up the cry, "Spank them buns!"

"Whip their arses purple!"

"Spank the bitches!"

Jed and Sam spanked away at the two wriggly bottoms presented in front of them. Four soft buttocks wobbled as the hairbrushes were brought down time and again against naked flesh. Laura and Sally squealed and wailed, begged for leniency, and shifted their bums as smartly as they could, desperately hoping to avoid the heavy spanks that were raining down.

Both girls were soon sobbing uncontrollably, their fingernails digging into the wooden table-top, their faces wet with beer and tears, their bare bottoms hot and burning.

Then without warning, they were hauled into a standing position, pulled away from the table and swung around. Laura was presented with a view of Sally's red-raw bottom. The tops of her friend's thighs were also crimson, where her wriggling had no doubt caused Jed to miss his aim.

Laura's own thighs were stinging and, as it dawned

on her that her own bottom and upper legs would be similarly red, she found herself being dragged across Sam's knee. Lowered over the waiting lap, the American saw her friend's frantically threshing body being placed in a similar position over Jed's knee.

The cheeks of Laura's face blushed red as she saw Sally being readied. Her friend's face was pressed against the floor to one side of her punisher, her legs held and pulled apart by willing helpers. The position raised her spanked bottom and caused her buttocks to fold open. Laura could see Sally's fleshy pink vagina and the thick growth of dark hair that peeked out from her bottom cleft.

She herself was similarly positioned, and knew that her own cunt was beautifully exposed to the audience's view. What was more, given the fact that her own bum cleft was hairless, she suspected the crowd also had a clear sight of her asshole.

Jed and Sam started to spank the two girls again, slapping away at their already sizzling bottom flesh with their huge palms. Sally and Laura began to howl almost immediately. Their legs were firmly held in position—spread wide—reducing their ability to kick and wriggle, and ensuring their bottom-clefts were kept nicely open. The two farmhands applied hard slaps to the clefts, fingers stinging the glistening pinkness of the girls' fleshy love slots and the wrinkled brownness of their puckered anuses.

"Fuck their tight little bumholes!" squealed the cider-drinker. "Let's put them back over the table and shag their cunts and fuck their bums!"

"You'll have a bit of difficulty doing that, won't you, Carol?" whooped one of the locals. "Unless there's more in those pants of yours than you're letting on!" The assembled throng hooted so wildly that, for an instant, their laughter almost drowned out the sound of the farm worker's palms slapping against the girl's naked bottoms.

Almost, but not quite.

"Put their mouths to work on the women's pussies, that's what I say!" offered a grubby adolescent, "While the menfolk fuck them both, in their cunts and crappers!"

As suddenly as they'd been tumbled across their punishers' laps, the two were hauled to their feet again. Strong hands gripped them and tugged them back to the tables, where they were once more turned over the beer-drenched surfaces.

"Go on, lads!" urged an excited female voice. "Have some fun with their lovely pink cunts!"

Sally's sobs turned into an anguished wail. She lay across the table, her face and blouse soaked in beer, powerful hands weighing down on her, pinning her to the wet wood, and prayed for the nightmare to end. Her skirt was wrenched down over her hips and thighs and pulled from her legs. Hands tugged at her tights and panties, fluttering at half-mast at her knees. Long sharp fingernails shredded the nylon. The sudden realisation that she was being undressed by other women made the ordeal seem even worse.

As the womenfolk stripped away the encumbrance of Sally's knotted clothing, and the men swigged their pints of ale, Maggie purposefully unfastened first Jed's, then Sam's, trousers. More whoops of delight echoed around the dingy bar.

The naked landlady pulled at Jed's cords, and as she wrenched them down to expose his powerful buttocks and thick, erect sex muscle, the cider-drinking Carol did the same to Sam. The two local women each took a penis in their hand and began to gently massage the rampant manhoods.

"Give it to 'em, boys," enthused Bill.

23

"Fuck their pussies!" howled the adolescent.

"Put it up their arses and fuck the crap out of 'em!" suggested a gruesome old farmer lounging against the fireplace.

Sally bucked wildly when she felt Jed's hands pressing against her scalding buttocks. "No! Don't! Please!" she pleaded.

The farmhand's thick cock slid inside her fleshy love-pot, ploughing through the slithery tunnel until his abdomen slapped against her bum and he was buried to the hilt. Sam's cock, fatter and longer than his companion's, made a similar journey into Laura's wet vagina. The American let out a high-pitched squeal as the thick length threatened to burrow into her womb.

"Now—fuck their cunts!" growled the gruesome farmer.

Laura and Sally stopped struggling. Pinned against the tabletop so firmly that they couldn't even twitch a muscle, they both realised, almost simultaneously, that their fate was sealed. The men were inside them, possessing them. All that was left was to take a fucking.

The cocks shifted inside the slithery holes, drawing back teasingly—as if to exit—and then thrusting forward, plunging into the pinkness, driving through the wetness. They withdrew again, and again they slammed home their advantage, diving deep into the slushy pink pots. Long, strong thrusts, terminating with hairy abdomens slapping against smooth, spanked bottoms, drew further hollows of delight from the watching crowd.

Jed and Sam thrust hard into Sally and Laura, riding the girls as if they were horses, their now-glistening muscles plunging into the exposed and juicy slots, hammering away at the tender flesh, working themselves towards a shattering climax. They pistoned ever faster in and out of their mounts, and as they did so, thick hands mauled the bare and tenderised bottom-flesh, thumbs dipping into bum-valleys, diddling tight little bottom-mouths.

Laura felt Sam ejaculate inside her, his hot fluid slapping against her vaginal walls. His long thick cock continued to pump juice for several seconds, and she found herself instinctively tightening her muscles around the throbbing manhood, drawing Sam's spend from him, just as she did with her boyfriend whenever they made love.

"Nice going, Sam," said Old Jack, as the farmhand pulled clear of Laura's dripping love-channel. "That should teach the nosey trollop a lesson!"

"Come on, Jed, you old sod!" It was Bill who was doing the urging, as the second farm worker continued to slam into Sally. "Give her your load!"

"Stick it up her arse!" cried Carol. "You'll come in no time up a nice tight hole!"

Laura heard Sally cry 'no!' Almost immediately—from the sounds, and the vibrations she could feel through the tabletop as her friend began to struggle—the American realised that Jed was going to follow the cider-drinker's suggestion.

"Hold the little bitch still!" Maggie snapped. "Get those cheeks wide open!"

Still pinned to the table, her face in a pool of beer but—for the first time since being stripped from the waist—her bottom unmolested, Laura heard Sally groan as her friend's anus was penetrated. Cries of delight and the clink of beer glasses confirmed that Jed had successfully impaled her.

Within a few seconds, Laura could hear the table creaking and groaning as the brutish farmhand thrust forward time and again, slamming into Sally, ploughing his cock deep into her bottom-hole.

Sally was silent now, and Laura could only imagine the suffering etched on her tear-stained face. All around, the villagers urged Jed on. The rhythmical thrusts, the creaking of the table, eventually stopped. Jed groaned and Laura knew that he was emptying himself into Sally's bottom. She was grateful that the ordeal was over for her friend. Grateful, as well, that her own assailant Sam had managed to come in her vagina—that she'd been spared the experience of having her virgin ass penetrated and sodomised by the callous farm labourer.

3

Her skin softened and cleansed by a relaxing soak in the bath, her long blonde hair—which had been crusted with sweat and mud—finally untangled by the ministrations of Debbie the maid, Lucinda Drake lowered herself over the edge of the bed and thrust her naked buttocks high into the air.

Slowly and methodically, her fiancé John then struck her quivering bottom six times with his whippy cane. As the long, thin rattan bit into her bum flesh, Lucinda buried her head in the silk sheets and sobbed. At the final stroke, while the pain was still coursing through her reddened buttocks, John muttered a new instruction.

"Open your legs, Lucinda."

He set aside the length of bamboo and unzipped his trousers.

"Do you know what I'm going to do now?" he asked, walking across to the bedside cabinet.

Lucinda continued to sob. Her bottom twitched sporadically as her caned flesh smouldered.

"I asked you a question," her master said sternly. "Please do me the courtesy of offering an answer."

"Fuck me," she murmured in response. "You're going to fuck me."

"Where am I going to fuck you?"

There was a pause, during which Lucinda squirmed uncomfortably against the bed. Eventually, she mumbled "in my arse."

She felt the sudden touch of his finger against her anus, gently dabbing the tight opening with cold cream.

"That's right, my sweet—in your nice tight arse. But to prove I'm not an uncaring lover, I'll lube your lovely brown hole for you. Your bottom is probably sore and burning from the penises you've already had inside it

27

today. Isn't that so?"

"Yes, master."

"Ask me nicely to fuck you in your bottom, Lucinda," John instructed, pushing his well-anointed finger beyond the ring of resistant bumhole muscle and up into her rectum. "Ask me to do it to you or I'll be left with no choice but to put the cane across your bum cheeks again."

Lucinda swallowed hard, and muttered from between gritted teeth, "fuck me in my arse—please, sir."

The bedroom door suddenly creaked open and Soames the butler peered in. Lucinda twisted herself over slightly at the sound of his intrusion, unwittingly offering him a sight of her fleshy right breast. Not that Soames hadn't already got enough to look at; her naked frame draped across the edge of the bed, her bare bottom criss-crossed with crimson weals, her lush pink vagina peeping out from between her spread legs—and her fiancé looming over her, his engorged cock throbbing inches away from her puckered bottom-crack.

"Yes, Soames?" the master asked in a matter-of-fact tone.

"Something of interest at The Birch Twig, sir," the butler replied impassively, unphased by the scene with which he'd been greeted on opening the door. "Two strangers, sir. Ladies. Mr & Mrs Leech have the situation under control, sir, but they thought you'd be interested to know of events."

"They were right!" John had already stuffed his erect penis back inside his trousers and zipped himself up. "I'll get down there straight away and see what's what. You attend to matters here, if you would, Soames."

Lucinda whimpered 'no'. She knew only too well what it meant. She knew her half-hearted show of resistance would be to no avail. "Her behind is already lubed-up if you want to take advantage. Do with her as you will. I'll see you later."

By the time she heard the roar of John's car's engine and the sound of its tyres scraping against the gravel driveway, the blond-haired, big buttocked Lucinda was draped across the lap of Soames the butler, squealing as his white-gloved hand spanked her bottom... then she felt the butler's thick penis slip into her backside. And by the time the master had pushed open the heavy oak door of the pub and stepped within, Lucinda's bottom had been flooded with the hot sticky contents of the butler's swollen testicles.

As she lay face-down on the bed, thick white spend dribbling from her anus, soft fleshy buttocks throbbing with pain, Lucinda reviewed the day's events and wondered whether it was all worthwhile. Whipped buttocks and a well-ravaged arsehole was a heavy price to pay to become the lady of the manor.

The door to the beer cellar creaked open slowly. The short, bulky frames of Bill and Big Maggie, who was now fully clothed, were silhouetted against a backdrop of dull light; light which nevertheless served to illuminate the features of the tall figure standing behind them.

Semi-naked, and desperately cold—except for her buttocks, which were hot and burning—Laura trembled at the sight of the stranger. In her present state, the last thing she wanted to see was a tall muscular man with a cruel face.

Sally sobbed and sniffled next to her, huddling in the corner of the dingy prison. Her back was pressed against the damp stonework, as if instinctively trying to protect her sore bottom from the prospect of further smacking.

"There they are, sir—the shameless bitches," said Maggie, "cowering in the corner like caged animals."

"They've had their arses spanked and their cunts well-

29

fucked," Bill chipped in.

"And the fleshier one's had it up her crapper as well," gurgled Maggie with a grin. "Old Jed reckons she had a virgin arse, at that!"

John moved briskly across the cold stone floor. His face was grim and threatening as he took the whimpering Sally by her upper arm and spun her around, in the same movement tugging up her blouse to reveal her spanked buttocks. As his fingers kneaded the soft warm flesh she began to sob more loudly, her body trembling and shaking uncontrollably.

"Stop blubbering," he warned, pinching at her glowing skin. "You!" he snapped at the American now, "What's your name?"

"Laura."

"Show me your buttocks," he demanded.

With no immediate way of extricating herself from the situation, Laura turned towards the stone wall, and lifted her blouse to her hips, revealing her pert beautifully rounded bottom.

The master continued to fondle Sally's bumcheeks as he admired the perfect shape of Laura's buttocks. He drew Sally backwards so that her body was pressed against his, his thick cock straining against the material of his trousers. Sally could feel it nuzzling at her bum cleft. "Did you enjoy your spanking, Laura?" he enquired.

"No!"

"Lesson number one," he reached round and under Sally's blouse, and began squeezing and pinching the soft flesh of her right breast. "My name is John Templeton. I own this pub, and all the land in this valley. Whenever you address me," he pinched at Sally's nipple, encouraging it towards a state of stiffness, "you will refer to me as either 'sir' or 'master'. So—I will ask you again.

Did you enjoy your spanking, Laura?"

The American was still holding her blouse at her hips, presenting her well-warmed buttocks to the landowner's attentive gaze.

She swallowed hard and bit her lip. This was a frigging nightmare, she thought to herself, and wondered what the hell she was going to do.

"I'm waiting," he said.

Avoid upsetting anyone, to start with, she decided. She swallowed hard again and opened her mouth.

"No… master."

For a brief second a sick churning feeling in her stomach became her overriding sensation, momentarily distracting her from the soreness of her bottom cheeks. She had never called anybody 'master' before; it was a curious feeling to do so. She was a liberated career woman, hard-nosed when she had to be; very much her own boss. Nothing in life had prepared her for the strange experience of acting so deferentially.

"Had you ever been spanked before?"

"No… master."

"Bend over."

Wondering if she was about to be spanked again, Laura tentatively leaned forward through a forty-five degree angle, barely altering her position. It was no more than a gesture, yet her reticence to properly comply with her 'master's' command was more born out of anxiety and embarrassment than wilfulness.

"All the way," he growled, and Laura knew he meant what he said. "Clasp your ankles."

She did as she was told, bending her knees a little to achieve the desired position. Her soft silk blouse responded to gravity and slid further along her back. She blushed, aware that the undersides of her breasts were now on view.

31

"Good girl," said John, admiring the suddenly cleaved moon of Laura's bum. The light in the cellar was too dim for him to make out the detail of her pink sex lips and brown anus, but the dark valley of her bottom cleft was alluring nonetheless, encouraging him to imagine stroking its clammy flesh.

His cock throbbed against Sally's bottom as he eyed Laura's beautifully presented buttocks. The sobbing woman squealed as his hands mauled harder at her big breasts, his fingers kneading her bullet-hard nipples, enticing them to thrust ever more proudly forward.

Without warning, he swung Sally around so that she was facing him and forced her down to her knees on the cold stone floor. "No," she murmured, as he tugged his thick erection from the confines of his trousers. "No, please…"

His hands wrestled momentarily with the thick leather belt wrapped around his waist, and then tugged it free, wrapping its buckled end around his knuckles.

"Then I will whip Laura on her buttocks," he announced. "And I will continue to flay her ripe arse until you change your mind."

Peering back through her legs, Laura could see Sally cowering before John Templeton, and knew what he expected her friend to do. She bit hard on her lip as she awaited Sally's decision. Her buttocks involuntarily clenched and unclenched in anticipation of the first stroke of the man's leather belt.

She watched as Sally took hold of the landowner's thick cock in her slight hand and tentatively shifted her weight forward. Laura couldn't help but be relieved at her friend's decision, thankful that her own bottom would be spared a dose of the master's belt.

Sally's body convulsed with sobs as she pressed her lips against the very tip of Templeton's rigid sex muscle.

Even as the tears streamed down her face, Sally did what was expected of her, fingers gently peeling back the foreskin—stretched tight as a drum across the swollen glans—tongue flicking at the newly exposed head.

Then she engulfed it, sucking on the stiffened cock. Her hand massaged its hairy base; her tongue and lips caressed its full length. Her head bobbed gently backwards and forwards as she worked her mouth up and down the veiny length.

Laura was fascinated by the scene. What she couldn't understand was why, as she gazed back between her own legs, a strangely thrilling sensation was coursing through her, as if she was in some way turned-on by what she was witnessing.

The master's hands were pressed against Sally's head, fingers clasping her soft dark hair, belt dangling against her shoulder. He was gently steering her head backwards and forwards, encouraging her to suck at his glistening cock with a slow, rhythmical motion.

Laura could tell that his breathing was becoming more laboured. He was pulling and tugging at Sally's hair with an ever-greater enthusiasm, and even from her curious vantage point—staring upside-down between her own legs—the American could see that her friend was becoming increasingly distressed.

Before long, Templeton groaned—and at virtually the same instant, Sally choked and whined. The landowner emptied himself into her mouth. His thick fluid trickled down her chin and dripped onto her big, milky-white breasts.

"Lick the cock clean," he ordered, nudging the twitching beast against the back of the woman's throat as encouragement. "Tickle the balls while you do so."

Sally did as instructed, sharp fingernails teasing the still-swollen testicles that lurked beneath a fine layer of wispy hair. Her chin was glistening with Templeton's come, globules of the thick fluid hanging from her lip.

"That is the last time you will spill any," he informed her. "The next time I afford you the honour of providing me with sexual gratification," he patted the leather belt against the palm of his hand, "you will swallow every last drop. Now stand up."

Sally knew better than to defy the stern master's command. Wet breasts swaying gently, she staggered to her feet, barely having time to compose herself before Templeton barked a further instruction. "Bend over the edge of that empty beer barrel."

Sally's face screwed into a grimace and a fresh stream of tears tumbled from her eyes. "You!" he growled at Laura. "Stand up!"

The American did as she was told, feeling a wave of relief as her blouse tumbled back into place, concealing all but the lowest portion of her bottom.

Templeton's expression was grim. He scowled at Sally from beneath a deeply furrowed brow. "Are you going to do as I say?" His tone demanded an answer from Sally. He rapped the belt against his hand once again and stared coldly at the sobbing girl.

"Better do what he says, honey," Laura advised. The American recognised an impossible situation when she saw one. Bill and Maggie were still standing to either side of the doorway, guarding the exit. Even if the two of the two friends were to attempt an escape, they were sure to find the front door to the pub securely locked and bolted. And who knew where the keys to Sally's car were; presumably upstairs, tucked away in the pocket of some savagely discarded item of clothing. No—for the moment, there was only one thing to do, and that was to comply.

"Go on, honey," she urged. "Bend over the barrel."

"Your friend's giving you sound advice," Templeton confirmed. "Do as I say, or it'll be the worse for both of you."

Sally wiped her tear-streaked face. Her sobs increased as she accidentally brushed her hand against the sticky white fluid plastered to her chin. She shuffled across to the nearby barrel and bent over its edge. The posture meant that her upper body was concealed from view inside the barrel, her palms resting against its wooden bottom.

In her newly adopted position, her buttocks were the highest part of her body, swelling outwards and upwards provocatively. Her cheeks peeled apart slightly, and though the flesh of her sex and bumhole remained concealed, the shadowy valley that cleaved her throbbing cheeks was alluringly accessible.

"If you'd swallowed like a good wench," growled Templeton, "this wouldn't be about to happen to you." He was coiling the belt around his hand as he spoke, and continued to do so until a strip of leather two feet in length was left dangling free.

Even with her head and upper body concealed inside the barrel, it was obvious that Sally was still sobbing. "As it is," the man continued, "I am going to whip this big shameful arse of yours until I have flayed the flesh off it…"

4

After her treatment at the hands of Soames, Lucinda returned to the bath. She soaked in the water and while doing so, lifted her legs into the air, held her buttocks apart and pulled open her bumhole, hoping the bath water would cleanse the well-used orifice.

In spite of her treatment, she couldn't help the feelings of sexual arousal that gnawed away at the pit of her stomach. Nor had she any control over the flow of her juices. Her sex had been dripping wet when she'd felt it before getting into the water.

After clambering out, she fingered herself again and, as she inspected her bottom in a full-length mirror, found she was even juicier. Her well-rounded fleshy buttocks still bore the marks of the caning John had given her, and were now also blotchy and raw from the butler's spanking.

She bent her knees slightly and thrust her bottom out, causing her cheeks to fold open. Even the flesh of her bum cleft was red, imprinted with finger marks.

She rang the servants' bell and within a minute, Debbie the maid peered in. A small but shapely girl, her big brown eyes opened wide as she gazed at the soon-to-be mistress of the manor. Lucinda had made no effort to cover herself, in spite of the maid's pending arrival, and was standing next to her bed in the nude. Debbie had seen her naked mistress before—it was the curious implement in her hand which startled the small brunette.

"Don't look so worried," the mistress smiled, "as long as you're good, I won't use this on you!"

The long-handled object was oval in shape, approximately an inch-and-a-half thick and made from tough brown leather. Its surface was covered in tiny nodules, and from the way the mistress was toying with it, Debbie could tell it was also reasonably pliable.

"Do you know what this is, Deborah?"

The maid nibbled nervously at her bottom lip, and felt the hairs at the nape of her neck stand on end. She didn't know what it was called, but she had a good idea what it was used for.

"No, miss," she croaked.

"It's a spanking paddle." Her eyes glinted as she uttered the words. "It's for spanking the bare bottoms of lazy disobedient serving wenches." The gentlest of smiles was playing around Lucinda's soft, full lips. She was enjoying herself. "Have you been lazy and disobedient, Deborah?"

"No, miss," the maid murmured.

"But you have been careless, haven't you?"

The maid lowered her head slightly, gazing recalcitrantly at the plush carpet. "There was that valuable antique vase you let slip from those lovely little hands a few weeks ago, wasn't there?"

Lucinda gazed sternly at the maid.

"The master was too lenient on you, in my opinion… Tell me, Deborah, exactly what 'sir' did to punish you."

Lucinda was delighting in Debbie's obvious discomfort. The maid's ill-at-ease disposition was further evident in the flushing of her face; the constant, nervous readjustments she made to her black blouse and very short skirt.

"He put me over his knee and spanked me, miss."

"On your bare bum?"

"Yes, miss."

"Well, you were very lucky, Deborah!" The mistress spat the words, thrilling at the way they caused the maid to flinch. "If you'd been made to answer to me, you wouldn't have escaped so lightly. I would have taken you down to the coppice, had Soames fasten you to a

37

tree and used this spanking paddle to beat your naked arse purple!"

Lucinda allowed a few moments for her words to sink in.

As the maid continued to shuffle uncomfortably, the blond-haired mistress toyed with the gruesome implement clutched in her right hand. At length she asked, "Do you want me to paddle your buttocks for you?"

Debbie shook her head from side to side and forced the words 'no, miss,' from between her gently trembling lips.

"Then you'll be a good girl?"

"Yes, miss."

Lucinda nodded quietly to herself and felt a sharp stab of excitement within her loins. She could feel her juices flowing.

"Now, Deborah," she said, "I'm afraid I am going to have to spank you anyway, because I'm as randy as hell—but it doesn't have to be with this paddle. I'm perfectly happy to smack your bottom with my hand, just as if you were a naughty child. Would you like that?"

"Yes, miss," came the murmured answer.

Of course the silly little cow wouldn't bloody like it, Lucinda thought to herself. And neither, for that matter, would John—if he found out!

Debbie's silence was important.

"Now this will be our secret—won't it, Debbie?"

Debbie looked at her Mistress' stern face and shuddered. "Yes, miss."

"Good. Now come and bend over the edge of my bed."

Debbie moved hesitantly across the room, stopping next to the mistress and tentatively leaning forward.

"Bend properly," Lucinda snapped, "so that you're supporting your weight with your forearms. Get that bottom high up in the air, my girl. I intend to give it a thorough smacking."

The maid rested her forearms against the bed. The adopted position had the effect of making her buttocks the uppermost part of her body.

Lucinda placed the spanking paddle on the bed and tugged Debbie's short skirt up to her hips. She felt little shocks of excitement course through her at the exposure of the maid's bum. Debbie's panties were skimpy and high-cut, running along the cleft of her bottom but leaving her buttocks completely exposed. These were the type of panties the master always insisted Debbie wore. There were occasions, after all—during his day-to-day running of the estate—when John found need to punish the maid but was too busy to spare much time. By making her wear high-cut panties, he was able to entirely expose her bare buttocks simply by flipping up her skirt, allowing him to quickly and effectively warm-up her skin.

"Thrust your bum right out, Deborah!"

Debbie did as the mistress bade. Her new position effectively pushed the straps attaching her stockings to her suspender belt well out of the way, leaving her buttocks, thighs and hips naked except for the high-cut panties.

Without further ado, Lucinda began to slap the beautifully presented bum cheeks, delighting in the crisp sound of her hand cracking against soft white buttock flesh.

"Bad girl!" she growled as she smacked. "Breaking the master's antique vase like that! Well let's see what we can do to make sure you're more careful in future, shall we?"

Smack, smack, smack!

Her hand slapped haphazardly against the quivering

39

globes of flesh, stinging first one buttock, then the other, before descending across both frantically squirming cheeks.

"Oh yes!" Lucinda said breathlessly, "I'll make you smart, my girl! Bad, naughty little serving bitches deserve to get their arses spanked! I'll slap this naughty-girl bum for you, you shamefaced little madam—just see if I don't!"

Debbie was squealing and gasping as the spanks cracked against her naked hindquarters. She twisted and turned, desperately seeking some relief from the chastising slaps of her mistress's hand.

"Keep still, you little vixen!" demanded Lucinda, grasping Debbie more firmly around the waist so that she could better slap away at the wildly bucking buttocks.

"Get down! Get your head right down!" the mistress spat. "Get this disobedient backside of yours right up in the air, you shameless wench!"

Smack, smack, smack!

"Higher!" Smack! "Right up! Get up on your tip-toes!" Smack! "Higher still!" Smack!

After a while, as her sex began to tingle from the fast-growing excitement of what she was doing, Lucinda decided to peel the maid's high-cut panties down, so that every morsel of the young girl's bottom was exposed to her.

"Cheeks right up! Legs apart!" she snapped, slapping the maid's upper thighs to encourage her to follow the instruction. Debbie arched her back and stretched every muscle in her legs. She was already on tiptoe but knew she had to get her buttocks even higher. Her reward for raising her bottom was to have it slapped all the harder by the breathless mistress.

"Legs further apart! I want to see your ripe little cunt!" Smack! "Let's see how this nice deep bum-valley of yours takes a few choice spanks!"

Debbie squealed as slaps stung the wet lips of her sex. From her uncomfortable position, face pressed against the mattress, the mistress's arm encircling her waist to control her wriggling while she was spanked, the maid had a perfect view of her tormentor's naked bottom. Even as her muscles strained to keep her bottom high in the air, and her eyes watered from the stinging slaps being administered to the soft flesh between her well-spread legs, Debbie felt herself getting wetter. The sight of her mistress's bum, burning red from spanks and cane strokes, wobbling gently as she exerted herself, thrilled Debbie in a way she could never have expected. Her face flushed and she began to gasp as tiny stabs of excitement increased the tingling she was already feeling between her thighs.

It was the sound of the door creaking open that finally forced the mistress to stop spanking the maid. Lucinda looked up from under her long, blond hair, her lips parted in excitement.

Soames the butler stood at the door. His eyes fixed first on Lucinda—naked breasts swaying—and then on Debbie's bare, spanked bottom, partly concealed by the presence of the mistress's spanking hand, now resting across both cheeks.

"Well…" he said at length. Debbie scrambled to her feet the moment Lucinda released her, and tugged her skirt back into place. Her panties remained twisted at her feet. "The master will be interested to find out what's been going on here."

5

John Templeton arrived at a ramshackle old mansion just as the sun was nudging its forehead above a sombre horizon. He screeched his car to a halt, ran his long tapering fingers through his thick locks of black hair, stepped out onto the gravel path and moved briskly to the mansion's oak door. Taking hold of the monstrous brass knocker, he rapped it twice against the splintering wood.

It was a chilly morning, but Templeton hardly noticed. His blood was up; he could almost feel it coursing around his body, just as he was similarly aware of his heart hammering like a piston in his chest.

Two new women in the village! He could hardly believe it!

Concealed in the depths of a valley hidden from view, Rattling Meadow was a location you could only stumble upon by accident—and there were few enough travellers in the area anyway, let alone ones who managed to get themselves lost.

He toyed with his belt edgily as he waited for his knock to be answered, and momentarily recalled the way he'd wielded the thick leather only hours earlier; the satisfying thwacking sound it had made every time he'd brought it down against the squirming Sally's buttock flesh. Even in the brief time he'd spent with the two women, Templeton had nurtured a dislike for Sally. She whimpered, and he despised whimperers. For women like her, a future in Rattling Meadow would be bleak indeed. He hammered the knocker against the door once again.

Laura, on the other hand, was an entirely different proposition. She had seemed altogether calmer, more in control of herself. She was American as well, a fact that made her all the more intriguing. Sure, she'd done what he'd told her, but Templeton knew that she'd probably rationalised the situation and realised that, at that moment, in that circumstance, she had no alternative but to comply. He found himself wondering how she might behave in the future.

His thoughts were interrupted by the sudden creak of the old oak door as it was slowly opened. The man who peered out at Templeton was an enormous, shaggy beast, dressed in clothes that hardly passed for more than rags and having about him the sweet stench of still-damp sweat. He grunted grudgingly at Templeton before opening the door a further few inches to allow the visitor access.

"Is the Sinfinder home, Mute?" Templeton questioned, breezing into the enormous cobwebbed hall that was dimly lit by flickering candles and heavy with the scent of damp, musty air.

Mute gestured towards the gloomy interiors of the old house, and Templeton strode confidently forward with the air of a man who had been there before. He peered through an open doorway into a dark and dingy room. The embers of a fire were still flickering in the huge marble fireplace, and two candles, precariously fitted into silver candlestick holders, glowered impassively on a splintered wooden tabletop in the furthest corner.

By the fading yellow light, Templeton could make out the drawn features of a darkly dressed man resting against the crumbling plasterwork of the far wall. The man's face remained coldly inanimate as the landowner entered, his eyes fixed on Templeton but betraying no emotion, nor even the faintest glimmer of recognition.

"Matthew," said Templeton, gently nodding his head in greeting. His confident swagger of moments earlier was replaced now by the most tentative of shuffling movements as he edged into the room; he was suddenly unsure of himself. The excited pounding of his heart gave way to a dull thudding as his anxiety festered. He could feel the heat of his blood rapidly cool. Beads of sweat appeared on his forehead, ready to tumble.

He wished to God he didn't fear for his mortal life every time he stared into the merciless face of Matthew Hopkirk, the self-styled Sinfinder General.

At length, Hopkirk murmured the word 'Templeton', and his passionless eyes, black pearls buried in the meanest of slits, followed the visitor's cautious progress into the room.

The Sinfinder leaned forward, leaving the shadows. Templeton felt his heart thud even faster. What was it about this curious man that made him so fearful?

"What brings you to my house of sinners? Have you come to pay your debts?"

"There are two new women in the village, Matthew," he said. "Pretty ones. My people have them locked away at the moment."

The Sinfinder stared intensely at his visitor. Templeton could see the flame of the nearby candle reflected in his host's dispassionate eyes.

"Mute!" the seated man shouted suddenly. The shaggy beast who had answered the door to Templeton lumbered into the room, his eyes bright with an eagerness to please his master.

"Raise your snoring colleagues from their slumbers and fetch me the slave-bitch from the cellar."

The man-mountain shuffled from the room; the Sinfinder motioned to the wooden bench positioned on the opposite side of the table at which he was sitting.

"Be seated, Templeton. Will you take wine for breakfast?"

"A glass, perhaps, thank you."

"A bottle, Templeton. Why stop at a mere glass?"

The landowner took a seat opposite his sombre host, his edginess accentuated by his confusion. He had been offered wine but couldn't see any, and wondered if, perhaps, he was meant to fetch a bottle from somewhere; but within moments he was provided with an answer. The creaks and groans of the floorboards in the hallway alerted him to the return of the manservant. He looked towards the door in time to see a naked woman sent tumbling into the room. Mute and two other burly males—one of whom was carrying two wicker baskets, each containing a bottle of wine—followed immediately, grabbing hold of the woman and hauling her to her feet.

"Prepare her," the Sinfinder instructed.

The man holding the wine bottles snatched the candle from the dusty table-top; the other two, clutching the woman's arms, clasped her legs as well and hauled her face-down along the table, positioning her so that her soft white breasts dangled over the far edge.

Templeton was bemused by the speed with which the men worked. Lengths of cord were produced from somewhere and wrapped around her wrists and ankles, each limb then being loosely bound to a leg of the table. Short lengths of cord were fastened to each of the bottle-holding wicker baskets. The free ends of the cords were then tied to her breasts.

The woman groaned as the bottles were left free to dangle, swaying gently from her tightly bound bosom. Rough hands were at her hips then, raising her up while a shabby blanket was stuffed under her abdomen. Her buttocks were clutched, plied apart and firmly held.

Mute lit a candle. He produced from somewhere a contraption which Templeton had never seen before. Made from brass, it was shaped like a small dish with a hole cut out of its centre. The manservant eased three or four inches of the candle through the small opening and then handed it to one of his cohorts.

Templeton saw that the brass dish had been fitted in such a way as to catch wax as it dripped from the burning candle shaft. He watched as the base of the candle was lowered into the soft valley between the woman's wide-open bum cheeks. It rested against her bottom-opening for a moment, and was then slipped into the hole, pushed deep inside her until the base of the brass dish pressed against her buttocks.

Templeton and Matthew Hopkirk drank wine then, filling and refilling their glasses from the bottles that hung from the female's painfully stretched breasts.

The human candleholder shifted slightly against the tabletop, causing the flame to flicker suddenly and cast dancing shadows across the Sinfinder's malignant features. His gloved fingers reached out and clutched the naked woman's hair. "Move again, you sinful harlot, and I will stripe you with my cane from your shoulders to the soles of your feet."

Templeton felt his heart begin to race. He had seen the Sinfinder go to work on one of his 'slave-bitches' before, had felt himself tremble uncontrollably as he'd watched woman flesh being tortured by Hopkirk's heavy rod.

The Sinfinder had shown no mercy… now he guzzled the wine until both bottles were dry. The girl, her breasts relieved of the liquid's weight, lay more comfortably, it seemed to Templeton. The flickering candle had burned down to a half-inch above the brass dish, which was thick with melted wax. Hopkirk raised his sinewy body from the bench and extinguished the flame with his gloved fingers.

"Be rigorous with these new harlots, Templeton," he said. "They must come to me prepared for their life as compliant exhibits in my circus. They must be ready to be trained to perform like seals. I do not wish to waste time beating out of them their wilfulness... Mute!"

The Sinfinder locked eyes with the man-mountain lurking in the shadows of the room. Mute and his cronies lumbered forward, and at a gesture from their master, unfastened the wine baskets from the woman's breasts and withdrew the candle from her bottom-hole. Untying the cords at her ankles and wrists, they pulled her backwards, cruelly dragging her breasts across the splintering table top, and repositioned her so that she was standing on the cold stone floor, her upper body bent forward across the wine-drenched wooden surface.

She was once again bound with cord, her wrists fastened to the two far-sided table legs and her ankles to the near ones, forcing her legs apart. She whimpered and sniffled, her body visibly trembling.

Templeton felt she had some understanding of what was going to happen to her even before the Sinfinder reached down into the gloom beneath the table and picked up a length of heavy cane. His gloved fingertips gently traced a path along the woman's lower spine, teasing the skin with the delicateness of his touch until she responded with a sudden shiver.

"Such soft flesh..." he observed, his fingertip dallying at the base of her back. "Such sinful flesh..." Templeton saw Hopkirk's eyes flicker with sudden emotion; "We must absolve the flesh of all sin," he said from between clenched teeth, "we must drive the demons from this sweet young body until it is once again pure."

The Sinfinder's fingers trailed down from the girl's back, lightly stroking the white buttocks that he intended to thrash so severely. "We must flay the skin from this shameful slave-bitch's body!"

The Sinfinder gave a strange high-pitched moan as he swung his heavy cane through the air. It travelled with such force that even Templeton, standing at a safe distance, felt the draft its movement created.

Thwack!

The landowner closed his eyes tight at the sickening sound of the stroke.

A split-second of silence and then the woman's body bucked; the muscles in her arms flexed tight, the cords dug deep into wrists and ankles, and a fierce crimson line appeared across her buttocks.

The cane whistled again, slicing like a sword through the air.

Thwack!

Again the body bucked. The woman sucked in a great mouthful of air and quickly expelled it in the form of a horrifying whine. The sound was flecked with pain, tinged with fear. It sickened Templeton to the very pit of his stomach.

A second weal, flushing against the whiteness of the girl's bottom cheeks.

Thwack!

She squealed now, clutched in a paroxysm of pain. Templeton watched as her hands clenched into fists and unclenched again. Her head rolled backwards and forwards and her hindquarters twisted and turned, cavorting wildly in a desperate, futile attempt to escape the agonies that consumed her.

Thwack!

She tightened now. Every muscle was tense, and she howled unashamedly.

The Sinfinder's face was deeply etched with determination. In Hopkirk's eyes, Templeton spied a sadistic frenzy, bubbling rather than boiling—the girl could be thankful that she had not actually done anything specific to enrage him—but sufficient nonetheless to ensure he was giving little quarter with the heavy cane.

Thwack.

There was a dreadful predictability about the strokes before too long.

Thwack.

The buttocks continued their feverish dance; clenching, flexing and wobbling uncontrollably.

Thwack.

As they wriggled, the pink flesh of her swollen cunt and the pouting brownness of her anus flashed in and out of view.

Thwack.

The cumbersome cane continued to whistle through the air, cutting into the victim's soft bottom flesh with all the fury that the Sinfinder could muster.

Thwack. Thwack. Thwack. Thwack. Thwack.

When his work was done, Matthew Hopkirk wiped the glistening beads of sweat from his brow and muttered to his manservants. Once again they emerged from the shadows and unfastened the trembling body of the naked woman. On this occasion, they pulled her clear of the table and hauled her to her feet.

For the first time, Templeton had a clear view of her face. Her eyes were closed—as she drifted in and out of consciousness—her cheeks streaked with tears, but the visitor could tell that she was an attractive young thing, probably in her middle twenties. Her small, pert breasts bore vivid marks where the cords had bitten into them and her whole body, exhausted by her ordeal, sagged like an overloaded sack as she was dragged from the room. Her buttocks flared a raw red, the heavy stroke marks which the cane had made across her flesh seeming to glower angrily at Templeton.

"The wench was lucky I am so inebriated," said the Sinfinder. "My blood is up, I should have liked to flog her for much longer…"

He dropped the cane to the stone floor and sighed wearily, "...but I am too tired. I need to sleep. These women you speak of, Templeton—I will have them, but you must break them in for me. Be resolute, and mark their skin with the whip until the wilfulness has been beaten from them. But mind..." the Sinfinder raised a finger in warning and stared deep into Templeton's soul, "...I shall come for them soon. My circus begins another tour in due course, and I will want to take them with me. Break them in swiftly, Templeton."

"Rest assured, Matthew, I shall prepare them well for you."

"Of course you shall, Templeton. You wouldn't want me to call in my debt, now would you?"

The landowner felt himself bridle. Hopkirk would never let him forget the debt that was owed. Templeton hated him for that, but he also despised himself. A drunken stupor and a simple game of cards had cost him his home and his land; everything. And miserable wretch that he was, he had begged the Sinfinder to be charitable, and not to hurl him from his estate and his heritage.

Matthew Hopkirk had grimaced—a terrible, twisted smile—a smile Templeton had since seen darkening the man's face on many occasions, as he soundly beat his slave girls like the whimpering dogs that they were— and had given the landowner two choices; to assist him in his preparation of slave bitches for his bizarre circus, or to be thrown from his own land 'like a snivelling cur!'

There had been no choice to make...

The lord of the manor enjoyed the drive back to the village of Rattling Meadow. His route home took him along a series of winding country lanes and past various fields where sheep grazed and farm labourers toiled in the early morning sunshine. Even in his open-top car, the wind in his hair as he drove along, he could tell it was going to be another hot summer's day. Another day of sizzling temperatures that would make the sweat drip, even before he exerted himself by wielding the lash.

In truth, he was uncertain what to do with the two newcomers. He had enjoyed thrashing Sally the previous night, certainly, and his lust had been further fuelled by the beating he'd watched the Sinfinder administer to the young slave-bitch, however barbaric and sickening it had been. He was eager to sting more flesh himself, but had to consider how best to satisfy the Sinfinder's requirements. He didn't have much time to prepare Sally and Laura for a lifetime of gratifying Matthew Hopkirk, and knew it would take much more than the cut of the rod to subjugate his charges fully.

Besides, he had his own fair Lucinda to deal with, not to mention his staff.

No, on this occasion, Templeton thought to himself, there would be little choice but to be immediately and remorselessly severe with the newcomers. He punched out a number on his mobile phone and listened to its ringing. At length, he heard the gruff tones of old Bill, the pub landlord.

"Where are they at the moment, Bill?"

"Down in the cellar, Mr Templeton. Me 'n' Maggie gave 'em their clothes back, seein' as how it gets awful cold down there in the middle of the night."

"I want you to prepare them, Bill. I've decided to send them to The Farm."

Templeton heard the grizzly old landlord chuckle to himself at the other end of the phone. "Well, Mr Templeton, sir," he gurgled at length, "those two city lasses are certainly in for a surprise or two if you're sending them there!"

"No time to lose, Bill, the Sinfinder has need of them. So I tell you what I want you to do. I'm going to contact

51

Hans and have him come up to the pub to collect them. In the meantime, you and Maggie get them up from the cellar, and prepare them in the way Hans will expect them to be prepared. You have the necessary clothing?"

"Should be able to lay our hands on some, yes sir."

"Good. Teach them what they'll need to know, Bill. You know how stern Hans can be early in the morning. I'd hate them to get on the wrong side of him before they've even left your premises!"

Templeton finished the call and swung his sports car onto the long and winding driveway of his manor house. As he cruised along the narrow gravel pathway, he admired the magnificence of the rambling country pile in which he lived, and knew absolutely he would do virtually anything to keep it from Matthew Hopkirk's covetous grasp.

It had been a long night and he felt terribly weary. A quick word with Soames the butler to ensure that all was well and then to bed. If there were any bad behaviour to correct, he would do it later, after a refreshing rest.

6

"You've got to try and pull yourself together, honey."

Laura clutched Sally tightly by the arms and gently shook her. The English girl had spent much of the night sobbing uncontrollably, her tear-stained face a continual reminder to Laura of their nightmarish predicament.

"I just want to get out of this place!" Sally wailed. "I want to go home—why won't they let us go home?"

"I don't know, honey."

In truth, Laura knew only too well the reason. Quite clearly, their ordeal of the previous night was not to be the only 'fun' the villagers were intending to have with them. Not only that, the American was more than a little perturbed by her memory of their meeting with John Templeton. When he'd visited them in the cellar, he'd made her refer to him as 'master'. He'd also warned Sally against gagging when he came inside her mouth. Laura felt sure these were signs that he had some kind of long-term expectation of them.

Not that she could allow Sally to know how she was thinking. Sally was too distraught. Being made to face the prospect of a future spent in captivity, perhaps even in the very cell in which they were being held, would be too much for her to take. Still, Laura consoled herself; at least their clothes had been returned, allowing them to claw back a crumb of dignity.

As she sat against the damp cellar wall, comforting Sally, her mind wandered back a few hours. She recalled the image of her friend, naked but for her blouse and bent over an empty beer barrel. She could almost hear again the terrible cracking sound as Templeton's leather belt had lashed into Sally's bottom.

To her surprise—and discomfiture—as the belt had been repeatedly brought down, Laura had felt a strange

53

stab of excitement at the pit of her stomach.

It was hard to explain why.

Before the previous evening, she'd never witnessed a beating. Caught up in the trauma of her own plight in the pub bar, spanked and made use of in front of a roomful of baying, inebriated observers, Laura's mind had simply blanked. It had been a natural reaction, as she desperately sought escape from the reality of what was happening to her. It had only been afterwards, down in the cellar, that she'd first become aware of a sense of excitement growing insidiously within her—first as she'd bared her own ass for Templeton to examine and then as he'd layed into Sally with his belt.

As she thought back to the beating her friend had taken, she was aware again of a certain thrill; a feeling, maybe, that she had entered dangerous and, for her, unchartered waters.

The opening of the cellar door interrupted her thoughts. She squinted against the light and felt Sally snuggle more closely into her; a small, scared child clinging for comfort to her mother.

Old Bill and Big Maggie were silhouetted in the doorway, the stark bulb glowering from the cellar ceiling too dim to illuminate the two shadowy figures.

"This is your wake-up call," Maggie said sternly. "On your feet now, both of you!"

Sally began to sob more loudly. Laura clenched her teeth and resisted the growing temptation she felt to slap her friend across the face.

Maggie strode across the cellar and snatched at Sally's arm, dragging her upright. Laura required no assistance. She recognised, as she had done the night before, that for the time being there was nothing to do but comply.

"Out the door and follow Bill up the stairs. Any trouble and we'll tickle your arses for you."

It was a relief to leave the cold mustiness of the cellar. The shaft of sunlight illuminating the rickety staircase temporarily blinded the two girls. The red-faced landlord led them back into the bar, scene of their humiliation the night before. On her way through, Laura glanced towards the front door. Inevitably, she found it to be bolted.

"Clothes off, ladies," Maggie shouted, as Bill reached for a pile of rags draped across the pub bar. He dropped them to the floor at Laura's feet, "and get those on. Be quick about it. We haven't much time and we don't want to keep Hans waiting."

Who the hell was Hans?

"Clothes off, I said!" Maggie spat, the venom contained within her words enough to fuel a further outburst of sobs from Sally. "And don't bother folding them neatly. I'll be throwing them on the fire tonight. You won't need them again where you're going."

"For pity's sake!" Laura exclaimed. The anger in her voice threatened to be drowned out by the sound of Sally's sobs. "This is kidnap—you know that, don't you? You can't just hold us against our will like this. You're breaking the law!"

"Ain't no law but the master's round here," Bill said gruffly. "He's the bloke what decides. Now do as Maggie says and get them clothes off. Hans will be here soon, and he'll expect to find you ready."

Laura voiced her earlier thought, "Who the hell is Hans?"

"You'll find out soon enough. Come on," Maggie clapped her huge hands together by way of encouragement, "you can either make this easy on yourselves or difficult. Either way's fine by me and Bill, but one way or the other, you will take your clothes off."

The two friends slowly began to remove the few items

of clothing that had been returned to them. Tights and stockings had gone astray, presumably having been torn and shredded during the events of the previous night. Laura's suspender belt was missing too, and they'd both been divested of their bras on Templeton's orders. In hardly any time, they were both naked.

Maggie flung some rags at them. "Get those on, then stand up straight."

Laura and Sally did as they were told. The rags turned out to be short loose fitting tops—the sleeves of which had been clumsily torn away, and which, in length, only just reached their navels—and baggy elasticated shorts that came to halfway down their thighs. They were each handed a pair of open sandals.

"Good girls," Maggie said, in a noticeably softer tone of voice. The big redhead eyed them up and down. With Bill now also giving them the once-over as he slouched against the bar, a freshly pulled pint of ale in his hand, Laura felt distinctly like an animal being paraded in a marketplace.

"Now listen to me carefully." Big Maggie eased herself onto a bar stool, took her husband's ale from his gargantuan hand and gulped expansively from the glass. "You're no doubt wishing you were somewhere else right now," she began. "That's tough, because you're here and you're here to stay."

Laura was hardly surprised to hear an agonised wail escape Sally's lips as Maggie's words hit home.

"No amount of blubbering is goin' to change that fact, so you'd better brave up and brave up fast. The master don't like crybabies—and neither does Hans. So sort yourselves out."

She swigged mightily again and wiped the froth that collected round her mouth. "From now on, you obey every instruction given you—that way, you'll suffer less.

There's one instruction, one command above all others, that you'd better get used to responding to…" she paused for effect "… and that command is—'present'."

She took another swig and stood up, handing the glass back to her husband, who promptly refilled it.

"To 'present'," she uttered the words carefully, "is not a command you want to hear. How often you hear it is up to you—but when you do hear it…" again she paused, and stared coldly into Laura's dark eyes, "…this is what you do: immediately clasp the elasticated waistband of your shorts with both hands and lower them quickly to your ankles, keeping hold of them all the time. Do not—and I repeat, do not—let go of them, do not allow gravity alone to lower them. Keep hold of them all the way down. When you have dropped your shorts to the floor, then, without moving your feet in any way, clasp your ankles and hold that position until you are told otherwise."

Laura felt her throat dry. The whole notion was preposterous. What was she, a fucking robot? A frigging dog listening for its master's instructions?

"Hans will expect you to be fast and efficient at following through this command, and he'll expect it from the word go—which means we'd better practise."

This couldn't be happening, Laura thought to herself. It was beyond belief. So now she was going to have to rehearse taking her pants down for some mysterious fucking guy with a German name?

"When I say 'present', both of you grab hold of your shorts and do as I told you."

Sally continued to tremble and sniffle next to Laura. The American was angry; angry at the way she was being treated, and angry at Sally. The snivelling little bitch. Laura almost wished Templeton would suddenly appear again and beat hell out of the crybaby's buns with his big leather belt.

"Present!"

The word acted like a starting pistol, firing a shot of pure adrenaline through Laura. Angry though she felt, her logic again told her to comply—because there was really nothing else she could do. So, her face flushed with rage, she gripped hold of the waistband of her shorts and tugged them down her legs, depositing them at her feet and then clutching hold of her ankles, just as Maggie had told her to do.

The blood rushed to her head. She'd been careful not to move her feet, which were no more than six inches apart—so for her to deposit her pants and clutch hold of her own ankles, she'd had to bend her knees. And it was that position—pants at her feet, hands clutching ankles, knees bent and naked ass thrust up in the air—that she grimly retained while Maggie strolled backwards and forwards in front of her and Sally, leisurely guzzling from a fresh glass of beer.

"You," the redhead muttered at length, "the tearful one; what's your name?"

"Sa-Sally," came the choked response.

"You're too slow. Pull your shorts up, both of you, and let's try again."

Stupid bloody bitch, thought Laura. As though the act of pulling their pants down wasn't humiliating enough, pathetic sobbing Sally had now caused them to have to do the whole bloody routine again.

"Present!"

Hands at the waistband; shorts, down the legs; hands clutching ankles; bums in the air.

"Too slow! Shorts up, let's go again.

"Present!"

Laura ripped the shorts down her legs, her thumbnails scratching the flesh of her thighs in her desperation to ensure she wouldn't have to repeat the procedure. She gripped her ankles tightly and prayed that Sally had presented her bum with equal swiftness.

"Better that time—both of you. But I'm afraid it's got to be shorts up for another try. When Hans commands you to 'present', he will expect you to offer him a pair of lovely white buttocks almost before he's had time to draw breath. On hearing that command, you must have no thought but to expose your bottom to him."

"Fucking Hell," Laura mumbled under her breath, feeling as though her situation was becoming more surreal with every passing moment.

"That attitude of yours is going to get you into a whole lot of trouble, Yankee girl!" snapped Maggie. "I'm trying to help you here, but you are both trying my patience." The redhead let out a sigh of exasperation and ran her fingers through her thick locks of hair. "Fact," she said sharply, "Hans is coming for you any moment. Fact; he will expect you—here, in this room—to 'present'. Fact; if you do not 'present' to his satisfaction, he will beat your bottoms so hard you'll be pissing onto those shorts in no time at all. Now, I know what he expects and I can help you satisfy those expectations. Or you can take your chances. The choice is yours."

Laura's stomach was churning violently as she anticipated her possible fate. Beaten so savagely on the ass she pissed herself? What kind of man was this Hans? He got his kicks from making girls drop their pants and then beating their asses nine shades of purple!? The American felt sick to the very core. A fact that made it all the harder to reconcile the strange tingling of excitement she was starting to feel between her legs.

"Present!"

Hands clutched at elasticated waistbands, material slid down soft flesh, slender fingers clasped slim ankles, and four bare buttocks thrust upwards at the ceiling.

"Good!" bellowed an honestly delighted Maggie. Laura could hear Bill chortling to himself behind the bar—the first time since they'd been 'presenting' that she'd heard any noise from him, other than a contented guzzling as he slaked his prodigious thirst.

They must have done it right.

A terrible pounding on the great oak door of the tavern made everybody's heart miss a beat.

"It's him!" Bill exclaimed, sloshing ale down his shirt in his haste to answer the heavy knocking.

"Quick! Shorts up, girls!" snapped Maggie, clicking her fingers as an extra incentive to Laura and Sally. "Keep a civil tongue in your head, Yankee girl, and make sure your friend doesn't snivel. And don't speak until you're spoken to!"

Laura could hardly manage to breathe. She felt clammy and sick, and was certain her heart was going to pound its way out her chest at any second. From the corner of her eye, she could see the trembling figure of Sally, gripped by fear, streaming tears. She resolved to be as courageous as she could, react to the dreaded commanded as swiftly as she could, and hope to God that if—no, when—Sally was slow to 'present', the terrible Hans was just and fair and didn't beat the skin off both their asses.

"Hans."

"Ja, Bill, good to see you." The accent was unmistakably German. Laura was well-travelled and had spent a considerable amount of time in Berlin. The voice was deep and sonorous, the style of speech disconcertingly clipped.

"Where are they?"

"Through there in the bar."

The trudge of heavy feet across stone slabs and the sound of the bar room door creaking on its hinges as it was hurled open was the only warning the girls had. Laura saw a flash of flaxen hair, the stern lines of a grim face frowning behind small, circular glasses, a second, shorter figure following up the rear, and heard the sonorous voice boom the word, 'present!'

Again from the corner of her eye, Laura saw Sally fumbling with the waistband of her shorts, and quietly cursed her friend. Her own hands clutched and swiftly ripped down her garment. Her fingers clasped her ankles.

Almost immediately, the German spoke again. "Shorts up!"

She snatched at the material and pulled the garment back up her legs, over her bum and her hips. As she stood there, chest heaving from a combination of exertion and raw fear, Laura was able to take a closer look at the newcomer. Hans was an enormous man, standing almost as high as the ceiling. Broad-shouldered, his face dark and ashen, he was wearing a sweat-stained shirt, tight-fitting trousers that hardly concealed the thick bulge at his crotch, and knee-high leather boots.

In his right hand he was holding a vicious-looking crop.

Standing just behind him was one of the ugliest boys Laura could ever remember seeing. A sallow, oily face, clustered with pimples, framed a pair of thick glasses; lank, greasy hair flopped haphazardly across a broad expanse of pockmarked forehead, and a row of uneven yellowing teeth protruded from a twisted little mouth. Soft, fluffy hair sprouted randomly along the boy's jaw.

"You are…?" Hans pointed the riding crop directly at Sally, who murmured her name. "And You…?"

"Laura."

"Present!"

Again the shorts came down. Laura felt her face flushing as she deposited the garment at her feet and gripped her ankles firmly. The size, the sheer magnificence of Hans' physical appearance added extra weight to his sternly growled command. She had reacted like lightning and suspected that, on that occasion at least, Sally had been similarly responsive.

Pants twisted at her feet, ass naked for inspection, Laura felt a dreadful shame overcome her.

That boy. What was that boy doing there?

It was difficult to gauge how old he was, but a teenager certainly; an ugly, acne-ravaged, buck-teethed youth, who'd just watched her pull her pants down for no other reason than because someone had snapped the word 'present!' at her! How pathetic and ashamed did she feel?

And now she was having to hold the position.

She could see Hans' and the boy's feet as they moved into the room. She and Sally had been facing the door when the command to 'present' had been given, so the newly arrived visitors had to walk around the two bent-over girls to access a view of their bums.

For what seemed like an eternity, nothing happened.

Laura, her head heavy with blood, could see Hans' and the new arrivals' feet through the gap between her legs. They were just standing there, inspecting her and Sally's bottoms. And with her knees bent and her feet some six inches apart, Laura knew the German and the youth would have a considerable view to admire.

She could feel the warm summer air against the flesh of her helplessly pouting cunt and her partly exposed asshole. She bit her lip anxiously as the seemingly interminable inspection dragged on. Her heart was still pounding in her chest, and to her left, she could hear Sally's shallow breathing as her friend desperately attempted to keep her emotions under control.

Why didn't something happen? How long would she have to retain her humiliating position while an oily adolescent's bespectacled eyes hungrily devoured the sight of her pink pussy and her naked ass, specially exposed for the purpose of his inspection?

Laura yearned to hear the words 'shorts up!' or even to feel the sting of the powerful German's wicked riding crop across her naked backside—anything to end that infernal presentation of her rear. She found herself almost willing the cut of the crop, hoping that the big muscular German would thrash her so hard that she wriggled and squirmed continually. That way, she could deny the oily adolescent the chance to fix his glassy stare on her bottom, to drink in its every feature until he knew each millimetre of her miserable ass better than even a lover could.

So what if she wet herself, like Maggie had said would happen if Hans went to work on her bottom? So she empties her bladder—so what? At least the kid wouldn't be raping her ass-flesh with his piggy eyes!

"Shorts up!" The growled command was sweet music to Laura's ears. The big German shifted into her field of vision, closely followed by his pimply apprentice. Laura could see that the boy's face was flushed. She was certain she could also detect the merest hint of a smile playing around the corners of his crooked mouth.

The little bastard had enjoyed his eyeful of ass, that much was certain!

"Hands on heads!"

Maggie hadn't warned them about this one! Both women followed the instruction with an admirable swiftness. There was something about this great strapping German; he snapped his commands with such confidence that compliance was an almost instinctive reaction. There was simply no question that they would do exactly and immediately as he had instructed.

Hans strode forward and roughly tugged up Sally's shirt, baring her breasts. His hands were at Laura's own garment then; one incisive motion and the big German had exposed her titties.

The pimply little bastard lurking in the background was sniggering quietly to himself, Laura was certain of it. She felt her face flush as Hans firmly gripped both of her breasts and gently massaged them. She was sure she could see the oily adolescent's glasses steaming up with excitement, especially when the exploratory fondling caused her nipples to harden like big pink bullets.

Laura watched the German give Sally's breasts a similar mauling. She breathed an almost audible sigh of relief when the muscular Aryan barked the instruction, 'shirts down!'

"You will accompany me now from this place," the awesome blond male announced. "You are to be taken to the Farm, and there you will learn to acquiesce to each and every command you are given. Do not cry, or you shall be given something to cry about; do not attempt to escape, or whatever freedom you may be allowed will be taken from you; do not be impertinent, rude, aggressive or obscene, or you will be punished more severely than you could ever imagine."

The German snapped his fingers suddenly. The oily adolescent pulled a metallic device from his pocket, stepped forward and knelt down in front of the two women. On closer inspection, Laura could see he was holding two ankle bracelets linked by a short length of chain running between them. The youth clamped one of the bracelets around Sally's left ankle, the other around Laura's right, effectively chaining them together.

"Follow me to my car!"

7

The dark boot of Hans' car was warm and sticky. Laura, her limbs intertwined with Sally's, Sally's hot, anxious breath against her shoulder a constant reminder of their close proximity, breathed a heavy sigh of relief when the short, bumpy journey terminated. Doors slammed, boots scrunched against gravel and the lid of the boot creaked open.

The big blond German loomed above the two women, silhouetted against the hot summer sky. He was ominously rapping the two inch-long leather tassel at the end of his riding crop against the open palm of his hand.

"Out from the car!"

The two women untangled their limbs and hauled themselves clear of the boot. They stood side-by-side— how could they do anything else? The chain attaching their ankle manacles rested on the dusty ground.

To their left was a large stone farmhouse; to its side an open shed, complete with timber sidewalls and a corrugated roof. Laura noticed the farmyard gate a few hundred yards behind Hans, leading out onto a winding dirt-track that disappeared into the humid, hazy middle-distance.

Laura suddenly became aware that the oily youth had disappeared and, ridiculous though it seemed, given her circumstances, felt an enormous sense of relief.

"Into the farmhouse," Hans growled, indicating a big oak door with a sharp movement of his crop. The two girls began to shuffle as best they could towards the building. At least Sally had stopped sniffling and sobbing, Laura thought to herself as they edged awkwardly across the yard; further pain and humiliation seemed inevitable enough without her pathetic blubbering pissing off the sadistic bastards even more.

"Present!"

That frigging word again. Instinctively, they moved to clutch their shorts. It took them a split-second to realise that, for once, the command had not been directed at them. Laura looked in the direction from which the instruction had been barked. To the other side of the farmyard area, in front of what, from its look, she could only assume to be a barn, Laura witnessed a scene that made her blood run cold. A small brunette, dressed in a similar short shirt to the ones which she and Sally wore, was clasping hold of her own ankles—about which a pair of shorts lay twisted. A hefty-looking farm labourer, his shirt drenched in sweat, was swinging a supple cane through a wide and dreadful arc, delivering swipe after vicious swipe of the terrible rattan to the girl's unprotected buttocks.

Laura felt her breath catch in her throat. The thwacking sound of cane against flesh tore through the still summer air, reverberating with an awful resonance around the dust-laden farmyard.

The girl groaned as the cane bit into her time and again. Even in the sunlight, it was possible to see the heavy red-raw weals criss-crossing her well-caned bum flesh, burning a fiery crimson hue. Each fresh stroke seemed angrier, more livid than the last, and Laura suddenly realised that here, at 'the Farm', there existed a code of cruelty more dreadful than anything she and Sally had experienced the previous night.

Perhaps what intrigued her most, as she watched the miserable brunette receive her punishment, was not the vigour with which the strokes were applied—a brutish farm labourer wielding a cane at a woman's specially presented naked bottom was unlikely to be merciful— but rather the immense resolve with which the woman took her comeuppance. Her groans were fearful, and it was clear there was nothing she could do to contain them—they were literally being beaten out of her. But as the supple rattan thwacked into her flesh, bending spectacularly with the sheer power of the impact, her body remained admirably still. Only the flesh of her buttocks moved, involuntarily trembling in response to each stroke.

"Shorts up!"

Instinctively reacting to the growled command, the girl dragged her shorts back up her legs, visibly wincing as she pulled the material over her freshly caned buttocks.

"Continue!"

She stooped down and picked up a huge wooden bucket, full to its brim with stagnant water. For the first time, Laura noticed the patch of wet ground near the spot where the caning had been carried out. Made to 'present' for the crime of water spillage—and not even fresh water! What a grim place the Farm seemed likely to prove.

"Continue!" The same word Laura had just heard, but this time growled by her own custodian, Hans. "I told you to enter the farmhouse. Do not make me tell you again!"

Laura felt a sharp stab of anxiety in her stomach. Both she and Sally had been mesmerised by the caning; had actually stopped in their tracks. They were lucky not to have received an order themselves to 'present'. Laura shuffled along all the faster in an effort to make up the time they'd lost. Maybe the truth was that Hans was quite happy for them to stop, to watch the caning; maybe he wanted them to know what was in store if they stepped out of line.

Sally was quiet and appeared unnaturally calm. Too traumatised even to sob, it seemed to Laura. The colour had left the English girl's cheeks, leaving her looking suddenly drawn and pasty. Laura couldn't help musing it was more likely to be her other pair of cheeks that boasted the rosy glow from that time onwards.

It was the gentle tinkling of their ankle chain that attracted the attention of the tall woman in the farmhouse. The great oak door opened out into a sprawling kitchen, its walls cluttered with various hanging pots and pans, its wooden table surfaces laden with trays of pastries and pies. The tall woman had been looking away from the door as Laura and Sally shuffled in, keenly observing the efforts of the three women who laboured at various jobs around the room.

Short blond hair, broadly shouldered; the tall woman wore a white blouse and a short leather skirt. Her long white legs were impressively curvaceous and attractively muscular, and the high-heeled shoes she sported marked her out as a figure of some authority.

She turned as they entered, revealing herself to be a high-cheekboned forty-something, with big, brown penetrative eyes, a long, angular nose and a tight, determined mouth.

"Gerda, my sister," Hans informed them.

"Present!" the tall woman snapped.

Laura and Sally ripped their shorts down their legs and clasped hold of their ankles.

"Shorts up!"

They tugged their garments back into place with equal swiftness.

"Not bad for newcomers," she commented, lending support to her considered opinion by the casual raising of her right eyebrow. "Have you told them all about their new life on the Farm, Hans?"

"Nein. They will find out soon enough."

"Then let me at least tell them about life in the

farmhouse." Gerda's mean mouth twisted into a devious smile. She folded her arms and sauntered towards the new arrivals.

"Inside this farmhouse," she began, "I am the mistress. If you find yourself working in here, then you answer to me and to me alone. If you are unhappy with the way you are treated by me, do not go bleating like snivelling bitches to Hans. He will laugh in your face. I am his sister and he trusts me to deal with you, in exactly the way lowly bitch-dogs must be dealt with."

She paused momentarily, her eyes flitting from Laura to Sally and back again, as though searching for signs of reaction to what she had said. Laura gritted her teeth. She remembered her earlier pledge to herself; to be as strong as she could. Sally was traumatised and ashen-faced; a defence against adversity in itself.

"There are certain differences between the way in which the Farm, in general, and this farmhouse, in particular, operate." Gerda's smile broadened momentarily. She turned away again and sauntered across the kitchen to the far stone wall. Reaching up above the stove, she took hold of an evil-looking implement and carefully removed it from the hook on which it was hanging. The long-handled object was made from a thick piece of leather, approximately ten inches in length, the final three of which had been separated to create two thongs. The very end of each thong had been trimmed, and tied in such a way as to create a small knot.

"This is my chosen implement of correction," she announced proudly. "You will find, if you are unfortunate enough to earn yourselves a punishment out in the fields, that the male overseers—including my dear, sweet Hans, here," she paused and smiled affectionately at her brother, "are somewhat lacking in subtlety, finesse and imagination when it comes to the disciplining of shameless, wilful bitch-dogs. I, on the other hand, being a woman myself, have a better understanding of the exquisite nature of flagellation. Allow me to demonstrate…"

Laura felt her heart skip a beat. Could this be the moment? For all the stripping and shameful 'presenting' she'd been made to endure that morning, she'd actually, seemingly against all odds, avoided any form of beating at all. The caning she had just witnessed had sickened her to her soul. The brunette had been made to 'present', in just the same way as she and Sally had been made to 'present'. The incident in the farmyard had really brought it home to Laura; the incisive tutelage they'd received in the bizarre ritual of dropping their pants was for one purpose and one purpose only—to expose their bottoms for a thorough thrashing.

Of course, Laura had known that from the start; you didn't have to be a genius to work it out. But to actually see it, to actually witness what came after the buttocks had been bared, the pose struck and retained—that had been a terrible experience for the American. Because now she knew how viciously the cane, or maybe the crop, or who knows what else, was applied to the victim's naked buttocks. She knew how gut-churning the ominous whistling, the terrifying crack of the savage rattan, would really be. She had seen how effectively the soft white flesh of a woman's bottom could be turned an angry, burning crimson.

"Esther, come here."

Laura felt instant, indescribable relief. Her stomach throbbed with a mixture of fear and excitement at what she was about to witness, but at least it wasn't her ass that was going to get it!

Esther was the shortest and whitest of the three girls

who were working in the kitchen. She followed the instruction her mistress had given her instantly—who wouldn't, thought Laura—and joined the tall blond woman at the kitchen table.

"I have chosen to demonstrate upon Esther," said the grim German woman, "because her skin is so white. It will show how effectively the knout performs its task. Here in the farmhouse, we do not use the simple instruction 'present' to prepare disobedient bitch-dogs for their just desserts. Here," Gerda turned towards Esther, and with the gentlest of nods, conveyed her expectation that the girl would follow the instructions as she announced them, "we say; 'remove'"

Esther, who, along with the other two kitchen workers, was wearing similar attire to Laura and Sally's, pushed her shorts down her legs and discarded them. She didn't clasp her ankles, as Hans expected the two newcomers to do, but instead returned to an upright position, exposing to Laura's gaze a thick triangle of dark brown pubic hair.

"Bench!"

At this next instruction, Esther paced across the room to a slim wooden beam, and promptly positioned herself face-down along it.

"And spread."

The girl steadied herself by tightly gripping the near end of the beam, and then carefully parted her legs. She lowered her feet onto the stone floor either side of the bench. The two other kitchen workers flitted across the room and swiftly wrapped cords around the girl's ankles. They then pulled Esther's legs as far apart as possible and fastened her ankles to metal rings fitted into the floor an equidistance either side of the beam.

" 'Remove', 'bench', 'spread,' " Gerda repeated, wandering across to the white, spread-eagled body stretched out along the narrow wooden beam. "Three simple instructions." She loomed over the young girl, playfully teasing her by using the vicious-looking knout to tickle her exposed lower back. "With one instruction—'present'—what do you get? Simply a pair of buttocks, positioned in such a way that to thrash them with an inflexible stick is the only answer. But with these three simple instructions, look at how much more you achieve…"—Gerda used the knout to indicate—"…the legs, stretched wide and out of the way; tied securely in place. Not trapped in a tangle of twisted material. The buttocks, taut, to increase the sting of the knout. And here, exposed by virtue of the stretched legs, the ripe pink cunt. And here, where the buttocks have been forced apart, the tight brown arsehole… the knout is made from thick leather, but it is flexible. It will curl into all the nooks and crannies of a bitch-dog's body."

The tall German woman elegantly lifted her right leg up and over the wooden beam, straddling it so that she was standing above Esther's head, facing the girl's naked bottom. The position caused her short leather skirt to ride up her smooth legs; exposing a further two or three inches of her muscular thighs.

"From this position, I can really work a bitch-dog over," she said. "I can whip the flesh of her arse; or I can bring the knout down between her legs. That way, the thongs flay the flesh of her pink cunt lips; the little knotted ends curl around and sting her clitoris. Or, if I want, I can aim higher, so that the strokes land here, in her arse cleft, and the knotted ends whip her arsehole. Look, I will show you!"

A sudden energetic movement and Gerda had lifted the knout over her right shoulder. Taking careful aim, she set about her task with relish. Laura winced as, first, the knout cut into Esther's left buttock, then her right, then her left again, slicing into the flesh, and causing the serving girl to strain and twist her lower portions against her ankles bonds.

"Wriggle all you desire, Esther. It will not make an ounce of difference. I will lash you, shameless bitch-dog, until I have flogged the flesh from your fat white arse!"

The leather whistled through the air relentlessly, landing with a sickening thwack on Esther's wildly jiggling bottom cheeks time and again.

"See how the buttocks tremble as they are kissed by the mistress's knout! See how beautifully the white flesh burns! And now…" Gerda began to aim her strokes at morsels of bum flesh near to Esther's stretched-open cleft, working her way in towards the girl's private regions with a skill and dexterity that Laura couldn't help but admire, "…hear how the bitch-dog squeals as I whip the flesh from her ripe little cunnie!"

A roll of the shoulders, the subtlest of upper body adjustments, and Gerda redirected her efforts at the grossly exposed area between the serving girl's wide-apart legs. Laura winced as the knout struck soft vaginal flesh. Esther bucked frantically, arching her back, tossing her head, twisting the features of her tear-stained face into a grotesque grimace of pain.

Thwack.

A second stroke, and she bucked again, hauling her upper body from the beam; soft breasts jiggled, scorched buttocks wriggled.

Thwack.

She hammered her forehead against the beam and begged forgiveness for her crime—whatever it was.

Thwack.

Gerda rewarded her with another hard stroke of the vicious knout against her exposed genitals.

"Squeal, you bitch dog!" Thwack! "Squeal for mercy! Wiggle those shameful fat buttocks as much as you wish! It will do you no good. You cannot hide your saucy little cunt from the kiss of the mistress's knout!"

Thwack!

Laura could hardly contain the tears welling in her eyes. It was as if she could almost feel herself the terrible pain that Esther was enduring, so keenly did she empathise with the unfortunate serving girl. Except, of course, she knew in truth she could have no understanding whatsoever of her suffering; no comprehension of what it was actually like to have a wicked sadist use a terrible leather strap against her soft genital flesh.

A numbing fear gripped her. Her fascination, her abhorrence at the dreadful floggings she was witnessing kept distracting her from the reality of her own situation. The truth was that she was no different from the brunette, no different from Esther. It could so easily have been her sprawled across that wooden beam, naked from the waist and cruelly spread-eagled. It could have been her howling and writhing with pain as the vicious German woman whipped her cunt with the knout!

Or how long would it be before it was she who was made to 'present' for some pathetic 'crime' such as spilling stagnant water, and uncompromisingly flogged with a heavy cane for her sin? In her mind, Laura knew there could be no escape from being punished; after all, that was why she had been sent to the Farm. The best she could hope for was to try and escape the kind of flogging poor Esther was enduring—a terrible, intimate, excruciating beating; to try and ensure it was only her buttocks which were punished.

"And now, the arsehole!"

"Thwack!

Gerda made another measured readjustment and swung the dreadful knout through an enormous arc. The thick leather disappeared from view between the swollen hillocks of Esther's buttocks. The serving girl gurgled and choked in reaction to the fresh assault. The other two serving girls stood side-by-side as the whipping proceeded. Laura could tell from their faces they were no strangers to Gerda's knout. There was nothing about their demeanour which reflected shock, or even horror; rather a satisfaction that, on that particular occasion at least, it was neither of them who had been presented and displayed to receive its ministrations.

As the tall German woman continued to bring the terrible knout down between Esther's buttocks, delivering with admirable accuracy the implement's knotted tips to the tender flesh of the girl's anus, Laura dared a glance at Sally. Her friend was as white as a sheet; her big brown eyes dilated with what the American judged to be a combination of amazement and sheer unbridled terror. Laura reckoned that, as with herself, Sally could only too easily imagine it being her own ass on the line.

Not a pleasant thought!

Eventually, when Esther's bare bottom had taken so much punishment it could barely manage to twitch in response to each stroke, Gerda lost interest.

Laura assumed the girl's increasingly subdued reactions as the whipping had continued were the result of some terrible numbness in her bum, though never having had a grizzly leather punisher repeatedly applied to her own ass-crack, she could only guess.

Gerda was panting heavily from her exertions, her small breasts rising and falling as she stood over her victim. Esther, her face hidden from view, her body trembling with sobs, whimpered like a puppy. The

German woman trailed the tips of her knout along the serving girl's spine, and teasingly used the knots to tickle her bum cleft.

"You see now how much more imaginative I am?" Gerda laughed, swinging her leg back over the beam. She snapped her fingers and the two watching servant girls quickly approached and busied themselves unfastening Esther.

"How glum you will be when you are out in the field, and a big fat overseer commands you to 'present'! How you will wish for the subtle kiss of the knout as you stand there, bending in the summer sun, your bums being blistered by the cut of a clumsy stick! How you will crave the kind of orgasm which this white-fleshed bitch-dog has just enjoyed!"

Was that the reason Esther had stopped threshing around, Laura asked herself. An orgasm? Surely not? Surely it wasn't possible that the terrible touch of the knout had driven her to such a pinnacle of pleasure as that.

And even if it had, the German was wrong to imagine Laura could ever get off on being whipped like a dog. Even so, the American couldn't help remembering the curious stabs of excitement she'd felt as she'd watched Templeton belt Sally's ass the night before. But that was different; that was all about voyeurism; being provided with the chance to watch somebody else's buns get a good seeing to. She sure as hell couldn't imagine her juices flowing once she was taking it on her own ass!

"Come!" It was Hans who snapped the word. "We have dallied here too long. It is time to take you to the fields."

He opened the farmhouse door and ushered the two captive friends out into the yard.

"See you both soon," Gerda light-heartedly called after them.

Out in the yard, another surprise awaited them. A horse and cart stood near the gate that Laura had noted on their way into the farmhouse. The sweaty farmhand who had earlier flogged the miscreant brunette was seated on the wooden cart, the horse's reins wrapped tightly around his hands. On the back of the wagon was a large cage, roughly fashioned from wood and held together by the considered use of various ropes. The door of the crude construction was wide open, and inside, Laura could see the miserable brunette who had suffered the farmhand's rage across the expanse of her buttocks. She was roped at the waist to two of the cage's vertical wooden bars.

"Into the cage," Hans instructed.

The two girls hesitated momentarily.

"Perhaps you would prefer to 'present'?" Hans suggested, encouraging them to remember the penalty for failing to comply with his every wish.

Laura and Sally did as they'd been told. Hans instructed them to stand with their backs against the bars of the cage, and then passed lengths of rope round each of their waists and through the bars, effectively securing them in preparation for their journey.

The sweat-stained brute with the reins encouraged the horse forward, and the cage lurched from side-to-side as the wagon pulled out of the yard and onto the dirt track. Laura wondered when they would next see Hans.

Their new companion's name was Margaret, and Laura won the woman's confidence by sympathising with her about the terrible beating she had taken.

"Do they whip you often?" she asked, fearful of the answer and yet, at the same time, feeling she had to know, to better prepare herself for what was to come.

"Often enough to ensure you're always sore," Margaret stammered, glancing furtively towards the farmhand. She

77

was obviously fearful; it seemed to Laura, that their communication might bring some form of punishment from him. He continued to steer the horse and cart, soaking up the summer sun and seemingly oblivious to them. "You must be strong," she continued in a tentative whisper. "You must perform every task that is asked of you, or your life will be made hell."

"I'd sure like to know what this is already if it isn't hell!"

"Believe me, it can be much worse. Keep your head down and 'present' when you're instructed to do so; that way, you're giving yourself the best possible chance of staying out of serious trouble."

"Where are we going?" It was Sally who asked the question. It was the first time she'd spoken since leaving the inn, and Laura hoped it was a sign she was getting control of herself, slowly but surely.

"To the fields," said Margaret. "We'll be put to work there. The farmhands will oversee us throughout the day and beat us when they feel like it."

"And then?" asked Laura. Her stomach was performing somersaults at the thought of being beaten.

"To the dormitories to sleep; then to work in the fields again tomorrow."

"How the hell do we get out of here?"

"You don't; not unless the Sinfinder comes for you. But you have to prove you're well trained before that happens."

"The Sinfinder? Who, or what, is that?"

"Shut up back there!" the sweat-drenched farmhand growled from between tobacco stained teeth, using his ever-present cane against the horse's flank to reinforce his displeasure at the women's talk.

The rest of the journey passed in total silence. The rickety cage groaned and creaked as the cart was bounced around on the uneven track, and Laura wondered how much worse their situation could possibly get.

Soon enough, she found out.

As the cumbersome wagon made its way along the rough road, an enormous fallow field came into view. Dotted around the huge open area were women dressed just like herself, Sally and Margaret, all engaged in various forms of backbreaking toil. The broad sweep of the landscape, dotted with animated workers, was further broken up at regular intervals by the unmistakable figures of the overseers, hardly moving beneath the blazing sun. Each of them held some implement of torture or other, clasped firmly in their hand, and moved slowly across the sun-baked soil, carefully watching the women who were in their vicinity for any signs of tiredness or slacking.

The horse took a sharp right as the farmhand steered the wagon to the gate of the field.

"Margaret, and two new recruits, Laura and Sally," he muttered to an olive-skinned colleague who was lounging against the gatepost, slaking his thirst with a bottle of cider.

"Always nice to have a couple of newcomers," the dark-fleshed gatekeeper chuckled, giving the gate the gentlest of pushes and watching it slowly creak open. Another crack of the cane against the horse's flank and the wagon was pulled into the field, bouncing and rattling this way and that as it made progress across the bumpy, dust-ridden earth. Before it had gone too much further, the driver brought the horse and cart to a halt and jumped down from his seat. Two other men, each wielding heavy lengths of cane, ambled across the field to join their newly arrived companion, who busied himself unfastening the women from the cage bars.

He removed the ankle shackles which Laura and Sally

had worn between them since leaving the inn, and then snapped his fingers.

"You!" he barked, fixing Sally with a terrible stare, "Step down from the wagon!"

Laura watched her friend's face crinkle into a grimace of pure fear, her body begin to tremble; it would be the first time since their horrific ordeal had begun that the two women had not been side-by-side.

"Go on, honey," the American urged. She knew her friend needed to respond to the wagon driver's instruction quickly; the two overseers who had come to meet them were both toying with their canes, itching to use them. The last thing Sally needed to do was give them an actual reason to beat her. She tentatively climbed down from the cage onto the ground, whimpering like a mangy dog about to be beaten.

"This one's to work here," the wagon driver said to his cohorts. "The other two are for Field Three."

Sally let out a wail, and tears began to roll down her flushed cheeks. Her big brown eyes implored Laura to somehow save her from her fate, to beg them to allow her to stay with the American. But there was nothing Laura could do, or would risk doing.

The door of the cage was shut and fastened in place once more. The wagon driver regained his seat, lashed haphazardly at the horse's flank, and the rickety cart proceeded on its journey, making slow but steady progress across the arid, uneven ground. Laura continued to hear Sally's anguished sobbing for what seemed an interminable age. She closed her eyes and tried hard to blot out the heart-rending sound of a friend in need.

Yet in the still, oppressive summer air, with not even the comforting melody of a bird song to cut through the prevailing silence, there were some sounds so terrible, they could not be blotted out. The distant, barked command to 'present!' echoed like a death-knell in Laura's ears.

By the time she opened her eyes and dared to look back towards the gate, Sally was bent forward, her shorts twisted at her feet. The bigger of the two overseers, his shirt dripping sweat, his bald head gleaming in the sunlight, was standing to her side, swinging his fat cane at her exposed buttocks.

And all around, Laura could hear the terrible, choking sound of her friend's anguished screaming…

8

Field Three was no different from either of the two fields through which the wagon had passed. A vast, yawning expanse of fallow earth, populated with women dressed similarly to Laura, all bending, stooping, trudging or straining at their various jobs, while muscular farmhands prowled around, wicked implements of discipline clutched in their hands.

Laura felt a dreadful knot develop in her stomach as the wagon was brought to a standstill. The two overseers standing nearest the sparse, brambly hedgerow by which the wagon driver had drawn to a halt came striding across the field.

The American was certain she could hear her heart pounding in her chest as they approached. She had witnessed what had happened to Sally back in the first field. It seemed sickeningly inevitable that the same would soon be happening to her. She clenched her teeth together and choked back the tears welling in her eyes.

"Be strong," Margaret murmured to her and, for a moment at least, Laura felt inspired by a fragile courage.

The opening of the cage door and the growled command of the wagon driver soon divested her of her momentary resolve.

"Out!" he snapped.

Margaret took the lead, as if she instinctively felt a responsibility to protect the newcomer, and dropped down onto the ground. She was immediately grabbed by one of the overseers, who proceeded to roughly pull her by the arm across the field, leading her to her place of work.

Laura lowered herself tentatively to the soil. Her whole body trembled gently, her nerve-endings tingling as she awaited her fate. Would she be grabbed and roughly manhandled across the field as well? Or was there something different in store for a new girl?

The brawny overseer who was waiting for her scowled from beneath heavy brows, impatiently rapping a thick length of cane against his own calf.

"Present!" he spat, with savage venom. How inevitable that command had been! Her hands were at her shorts almost before the overseer had finished uttering the word. Having expected the instruction, Laura hoped, at least, to impress him with the speed of her response. She ripped the garment down her legs as she'd been taught to do, depositing it at her feet and clutching hold of her ankles. She felt her stomach almost rise into her throat as she held the demeaning posture, and began to breathe more heavily.

Laura kept her eyes trained on the overseer's heavy boots as he wandered to her side, each one of his steps in the dust bringing her closer to her fate.

She knew now. She knew what was about to happen to her. It had happened to Sally and now it was going to happen to her. She was to be caned on her naked ass! Except she'd pulled the really short straw; she'd got some bastard who wanted to take his time. At least in Sally's case, the sickening sound of the first stroke had followed on almost immediately from the growled command to 'present'. Sal could hardly have had time to drop her pants before the opening stroke had landed.

Laura felt the bile rising in her throat, was aware of the sun's warmth on her naked ass...

...and heard the savage sound of the heavy rattan slicing through the humid air.

Thwack.

In the instant before she was consumed by sharp, searing pain, Laura's bemused mind struggled to reconcile the savage swishing sound with the heart-stopping sensation of the rattan impacting on her own flesh. In that single moment, she was made to realise that this caning was not like the others; that this time, the terrible cutting sound, as the heavy implement sliced the air, was terminated when it landed on her ass!

The pain of the stroke stabbed its way through her, burning deep into the flesh of her bare buttocks, making her lurch forward. She gritted her teeth, held her ankles more firmly and grimly resolved to hold the posture demanded of her.

Again the terrifying whistle as the overseer launched his cane at her bottom-cheeks

Thwack.

The cut struck higher than the first, biting savagely at the less fleshy portion of her bottom. She lurched again, and wheezed as an incomparable pain danced across her perfectly presented moons.

"Fuck!" Laura expelled the expletive quietly, within a huge exhalation of breath, and felt fresh tears well up in her eyes. She could hardly believe the pain she was suffering and felt certain of wetting herself if the flogging continued. She bit hard at her lip, and concentrated her efforts on controlling her bladder and her tears.

The overwhelming stillness of the sultry morning was shattered for a third time by a powerful slicing sound. The monstrous implement was once more propelled at her soft buttock-flesh.

Thwack.

Lower that time, on the fulsome crown of her bottom. Laura sucked in a huge mouthful of dry air as she felt the whole of her ass begin to smoulder.

Thwack.

Again she sucked in air. Another line of fiery pain burned the width of her naked hemispheres. She staggered this time, unable to find the same level of

resolve as Margaret had managed during her whipping—
Thwack—and was punished for her lack of self control
with a stroke that scolded her even before the intense
pain of its predecessor had run its course.

Thwack.

The fearful swishing sound again; then, the awful crack
as the vicious cane impacted on her already-scorched
bottom flesh; then a dreadful pain, lacerating her nerve
endings—and from her own mouth, forcing its way up
through her parched throat, a fearful, gurgling whine,
merged with a stammered plea for leniency.

Thwack.

No leniency was shown. More savage, searing pain
consumed her buttocks. Her flesh seemed almost to sizzle
as the barbaric implement of torture was brought down
time after time across the swollen, throbbing hillocks of
her naked bottom.

Even as tears tumbled from her cheeks onto the dried-
out soil, and her knuckles turned white, so tightly was
she clasping her ankles in a desperate attempt to retain
her posture, Laura couldn't help but imagine the sight
she was presenting; her shorts twisted at her feet, her
legs slightly bent, her bottom thrust out and up, stomach-
churning sobs escaping her wet lips—and all the while
a brutish overseer lacerating her miserable ass cheeks
with stroke after grotesque stroke of his evil cane.

Her bottom suddenly felt so big! Her bum cheeks so
swollen and puffy! Laura was no longer aware of
anything physically except her poor throbbing bottom,
and felt certain she could be no more than a couple of
strokes away from passing out.

The caning was proving every bit as terrible as she'd
imagined it would be. The rattan cracked against her
swollen nates once more, cutting into the tender crease
where her buttocks sloped into her thighs. Laura began

padding her feet against the earth, desperately trying to alleviate the stabbing pain burning the whole expanse of her savagely tenderised bottom flesh.

"Shorts up!"

The command came as she felt her knees begin to buckle. One more malevolent swipe of the heavy cane, and she would have tumbled to the cracked ground, and no doubt been flogged for the crime where she lay.

She hauled her shorts up her legs as best she could. Her arms were shaking and she felt dangerously light-headed. Her buttocks burned and smouldered, and the feel of her shorts against her well-beaten bottom flesh as she tugged them back into place made her grimace in pain.

"Come!" Another clipped and urgent command from the overseer. Laura followed her heavy-browed punisher out into the field, wiping the tears from her face as she stumbled along. It was a futile task. Even as she dried her skin, the uncomfortable touch of the material of her shorts against her throbbing bum cheeks caused fresh tears to well up in her eyes.

The brutish overseer took her to the area of the field where Margaret was busily digging out a hole in the rock-hard soil, and hurled a shovel at her feet.

"Dig!" he barked. He ensured that Laura followed his instruction, then, satisfied that she had no intention other than to comply with his every demand, he wandered away, absent-mindedly tapping his devilish rattan against his leg as he went.

"Well done!" Margaret murmured to Laura as the two women dug. "I saw them giving you that beating. You did very well. What you need to do now is to keep a low profile. The last thing you want at the moment is to earn yourself any more stripes."

Laura wholeheartedly agreed with her new friend's

opinion. Even so, she couldn't help thinking it was easier said than done to stay out of trouble.

As she dug, she looked around her at the other workers in Field Three.

Every now and again, there would be a growled warning from one of the overseers, or a snapped command to work faster. As the sun beat down relentlessly, and Laura began to drip sweat in a very unladylike manner, she came to realise just how inevitable further whippings were.

Within hardly any time at all, she had heard again, close by, the terrible, guttural instruction to 'present'. As she worked, she angled herself in such a way as to see the drama unfold. A tall, older woman—Laura put her at somewhere between forty and forty-five—snatched her shorts to her feet and clasped her ankles. Laura had no idea what her crime had been, but was already wise enough to realise it was possible that no transgression had occurred; that the overseer simply felt like whipping an ass. The woman's big bottom bloomed magnificently, offering a perfect and enticing target for the sadistic ministrations of her overseer. How whippable the bare bum looked, Laura mused to herself. She wondered if her own ass had also displayed that same provocative fullness, if her bum cheeks had parted in a similarly revealing way when she herself had been in the 'present' position.

The overseer lost no time in applying his devilish cane to the older woman's naked moons. It was the doom-laden sound of the rattan swiping the still air that made the American feel sick to the pit of her stomach. Laura thought it worse even than the heavy cracking noise the cane made as it impacted on soft flesh.

The older woman, who groaned as she was tortured, remained impressively still throughout her ordeal. The only movements she made was when the cane struck her bottom with such force it made her lurch forward, just as had happened to Laura. The overseer, a spindly sparrow of a man, was swinging the cane through an enormous arc in his delivery of each stroke. He staggered momentarily himself on the implement's every impact with the woman's buttocks, so much power was he putting behind the cuts.

"Shorts up!" he barked at length. The woman pulled the garments back into place, picked up a heavy sack of grain that was resting nearby, and proceeded to stagger away.

"Present!"

The command came from another nearby quadrant of the field. Laura shifted around again, hating herself for being intrigued by the terrible beatings her fellow workers were enduring. All the time, even as her heart pounded and her stomach churned in response to the scenes she was watching, she kept on digging.

It was an attractive young woman who this time proffered her bare bottom to the caress of the summer sunlight. The overseer who had commanded her to bend set about warming her flanks almost as soon as she'd clasped her ankles. Unlike his colleagues, he took a riding crop, rather than a cane, to his victim's buttocks. He worked her over with a style all his own, applying fast and furious strokes that made her wriggle deliciously. After he'd successfully stung every morsel of her jiggling bottom, he used the leather tassel at the end of the crop to tickle her beautifully exposed swollen cunt lips.

"Shorts up!" the punisher growled, once he'd tired of teasing her genitalia. The attractive woman replaced her garment and returned to her digging.

Laura sighed heavily and wiped the sweat from her brow.

"Dig, bitch-dog!" snapped the overseer who had earlier so mercilessly put the cane to her buttocks. The American felt a sharp stab of anxiety in her stomach at the sound of his brutish voice. Her bottom was throbbing from the punishment she'd already received. Another order to 'present' would have been more than she could have taken. As the sweat dripped from her, she redoubled her backbreaking efforts, eager to ensure her shorts remained in place.

The sun was shimmering high in the sky when a huge wagon, bigger than the one which had brought Laura here, clattered into the field, pulled along behind two powerful horses. A whistle sounded from somewhere, and all the women immediately downed their tools and headed towards the wagon. Laura was confused. What was the next ordeal likely to be, she mused.

"Lunch," said Margaret, encouraging the American towards the waiting wagon. "Do exactly as I do and you'll be okay."

Laura stood on the back of the big wagon with her co-workers, as it made its slow progress out of the field and along the pothole-laden track, and felt utterly miserable. The women who surrounded her were similarly grim-faced, but carried in their eyes what Laura interpreted as a shared look of complete resignation. She wondered how the others would be interpreting her expression. Would they detect the fear, the anxiety in her eyes? Was there anything about her that betrayed the peculiar, inexplicable sense of excitement that lurked within her?

She didn't know.

What she did know was that she was hungry, and felt a keen sense of anticipation when the wagon finally rolled to a halt. Under the instruction of the three overseers who had accompanied them in the wagon, the women dropped to the dusty ground. They had been delivered to a large open area at the back of the farmhouse. Laura could see the stern-faced Gerda in the distance, and felt relieved that the woman's vicious-looking knout was nowhere on view. Instead, the German wielded an enormous ladle, and was busily stirring some kind of foul, steaming gruel in a huge metal pot. The three farmhouse serving girls, one of whom was the unfortunate Esther, stood behind a rough wooden table, on which rested another two smaller pots and piles of wooden dishes.

To the left of the makeshift kitchen area, Laura could see rows of logs. Each was elevated—in a horizontal position about one foot off the ground—by the presence of two wooden supports, one positioned at each end. The arrangement effectively turned each log into a bench. Perhaps the most curious aspect of the crudely designed seating, however, were the five vertical, horn-shaped protuberances strapped to every log.

The women workers were ushered towards the makeshift kitchen. With all but Laura well versed in the lunchtime routine, the group made swift progress across the yard area. The American took her place in the queue for food, standing immediately behind Margaret, and wondered whether she might be about to enjoy at least a brief interlude from the threat of the cane. It soon became apparent that even lunchtime offered no respite from the horrors of the Farm.

The women in front of her each took their turn to collect a bowl of soup, shuffled to the end of the wooden table, and then dipped their hand into a pot which Ester held out in front of them. Their fingers emerged covered in ointment. They then made their way across to the logs, rested their food on the ground and pulled down their shorts.

Laura felt her stomach churn again as she realised that

even the taking of lunch would require her to bare her miserable ass once more. Anxious though she was, the American watched intrigued as each woman reached around and pulled apart her own buttocks, and then dabbed herself with ointment. They then each faced away from the log to which they'd moved, and lowered themselves carefully onto one of the upward-jutting, horn-shaped protuberances. Laura watched them gently readjust themselves before tentatively resting their buttocks against the log, picking up their bowls and beginning to eat.

"I don't understand," she murmured.

Margaret cast a furtive glance at her, and then quickly checked to make sure none of the overseers were paying them particular attention. "We take our food, take some lube, then go to the logs," she broke off as a brawny overseer strolled passed them. "Then we sit on the log-knobs."

"How?"

"Lubricate your bumhole, then sit down on one of the knobs so that it goes up inside you. The overseers like us 'secured' when we eat our meals."

Margaret reached the table, took a bowl of soup from the impassive Gerda and moved along the line to Esther. She scooped a dollop of lubricant from the girl's container, checked to ensure Laura was making good progress behind her, and headed for the logs.

Soup bowl in one hand, dollop of greasy ointment balanced precariously on the fingers of the other, Laura followed in her friend's wake across to the logs. She watched Margaret drop her shorts, pull her own buttocks apart and apply the colourless, jelly-like substance to her bumhole. Then, tentatively, the brunette sat down on a log-knob. Bowl on the ground, shorts to her ankles, Laura reached around to her sore buttocks and slid her

91

fingers into the cleft. She plied her bottom cheeks apart and, holding them open, dabbed her ass-crack with the lubricant.

"Push your finger into your bum," Margaret advised. "You'll need to lube right up inside. The log-knob reaches a long way in."

For the first time in her life, Laura slipped a finger into her anus. She quickly dabbed the warm, rubbery flesh in her rectum with the lubricant, eager to complete the task before anybody had chance to see her performing such a shameful act. Then she turned away from the log and lowered herself until her bottom rested against one of the horn-shaped protuberances.

"Hold your bumcheeks apart," said Margaret. "Get them as wide as possible, and careful when you lower yourself onto the log-knob; it's your first time, your bumhole's bound to be tight—unless you've got a boyfriend or husband making regular use of it."

Laura had neither a boyfriend nor a husband. Nor had any man ever done more than distractedly stroke her there. It was strange to think she was about to give up her ass virginity to a wooden horn!

She gritted her teeth, felt tears of humiliation well up in her eyes, and gently lowered herself even further. She pressed her bum against the horn-shaped object and, summoning up her courage, sank down onto it. It was the strangest of sensations. Laura felt the protuberance glide effortlessly inside her. The lubricant anointing her bottom-hole ensured the object's passage was relatively painless for her, but she felt well and truly impaled nevertheless. Margaret had been right; the log-knob reached deep within her. She shifted uncomfortably against her wooden seat, hoping to ease the curious sensation she felt of wanting to pass a stool.

"You'll get used to it," said Margaret. "It feels horrible

at first, but you'll soon get more expert with the lubricant, then it won't be so uncomfortable."

"I feel like I've got a tree trunk up my ass," Laura murmured, picking up her bowl of steaming soup. "What kind of sick frigging place is this, for pity's sake?"

Two of the overseers were strolling nonchalantly backwards and forwards along the rows of seated workers. As they passed each of the women, they stooped to check that she was correctly impaled on her anal plug. In every case, they seemed satisfied with what they saw.

"Just keep your head down, like I told you," Margaret whispered to Laura. "Do what you're told, when you're told, and you'll be okay."

"How long have you been here?" The American grimaced as she asked the question. Gerda's lunchtime soup was truly disgusting.

"All my adult life. I was born in the village, and brought to the Farm at the age of sixteen."

"Gee, it's a wonder you've any skin at all left on your ass!"

Laura surprised herself with the light-hearted nature of her comment. But then, she mused, she was surprising herself constantly. Why, for example, had she been so intrigued by the canings she'd witnessed? Not only that, but how could she explain the knot of excitement she'd been feeling in her stomach from virtually the moment she'd first been manhandled into the inn? And why was it that she felt curiously exhilarated by her latest predicament; made to eat ditchwater while seated on a log, her pants at her ankles, and what was—to all intents and purposes—a dildo, plugging her ass? And what about the tingle of excitement she felt every time one or other of the watchful overseers strolled behind her? What did that mean? Did she actually hope they might put a cane stripe across her bare buttcheeks as they passed? Whether she did or not, she remained unmolested throughout the ordeal of eating her soup.

Within half an hour, after swilling their bowls and being made to use scrubbing rags and disinfectant to wash down the anal plugs, the women had been returned to their field. The hard labour continued then, the macabre stillness in the air being regularly punctuated by the sound of the dreaded command to 'present'. Inevitably, further familiar sounds would follow: the whistling of cane or crop as it cut the air, the crack of rattan or leather against naked flesh, the pathetic whimpering of the bare-bottomed victim.

Laura's arms trembled as she dug, her muscles unused to the backbreaking work. She knew it was only a matter of time before one of the overseers—one who maybe felt too many minutes had passed since last he'd whipped an ass—decided he wanted to work her buttcheeks over. Margaret had already been made to drop her shorts and clasp her ankles. Laura hadn't dared look, even for a moment, as her workmate had been caned. Yet somehow, not looking seemed to make it worse.

As the sweat trickled down her face and her muscles strained to scoop yet another shovelful of dry earth from the still-shallow hole she was digging, Laura could hear the repetitive, remorseless sound of the whistling rod, its merciless crack as it cut into her new-found friend's ass cheeks, and Margaret's anguished, muffled moans; irrefutable evidence of her suffering.

The shadows grew longer and Laura's pain-wracked body began to stiffen from her unfamiliar physical exertions. The afternoon had been a kind of terrible torment; all around her the sound of swishing canes, the sight of blushing, punished bottoms, yet still she waited anxiously for the moment when she herself would have to 'present'. It would've been silly to make out that the anticipation was worse than the reality would prove to be, but at least once she'd had her bum beaten, she would probably be safe for a while, more able to relax.

Laura's nervous musings were interrupted by the arrival in Field Three of another rickety wagon.

"Here she is," Laura heard an overseer muttering to his colleague, "the stuck-up bitch."

Making certain that at all times she was seen to be digging, the American repositioned herself in such a way as to afford a view of the newly arrived transportation. She could see a woman with long blond hair, inevitably dressed in shirt and shorts, being manhandled from the makeshift cage on the back of the wagon. A number of the overseers had gathered around her and were whooping with delight as two of their number dragged the struggling newcomer across the field. They took the frantically resisting female to a large wooden cross, which Laura had first noticed on her own arrival. Positioned in the middle of Field Three, the object stood seven to eight feet in height, with the horizontal crosspiece secured at approximately six feet.

The woman was turned towards the cross and swiftly fastened to it, her wrists raised above her head and tightly bound to the crosspiece. Even as one of the overseers was securing her, another was pulling down her pants, baring her broad, ample bottom to the eager eyes of his laughing cohorts.

"Not so high and mighty now, are we, Mistress Lucinda!" yelled one of the sweatier whip-wielding beasts. "Let's see if this arse of yours is good for anything other than sitting on a horse!"

The assembled throng broke into uproarious laughter at their colleague's brazen wit. The man himself followed up his wisecrack by firmly gripping the woman's bottom cheeks in his shovel-sized hands, and proceeded to vigorously squeeze and wobble them with an almost feverish enthusiasm.

Who was this blond-haired newcomer? 'Mistress Lucinda', they'd called her. She was obviously known to them, and judging by their zealous reaction to her arrival, she was also somebody they were glad to have held firmly in their brutish clutches.

"The mistress of the manor," Margaret murmured. "She must've done something to displease the master."

"The master?"

"John Templeton, the landowner. They are to be married. She must really have annoyed him to find herself sent to the Farm!"

Although Laura continued with her digging, she had little need to do so with any great enthusiasm or diligence. Without exception, the overseers had been distracted by the arrival of Mistress Lucinda, and continued to watch the new scene unfold from their various vantage points around the field.

Lucinda's short shirt was tugged up over her breasts, and then pulled up over the back of her head, exposing the soft skin of her back and shoulders. Her right foot was lifted from the ground and the open sandal she was wearing removed.

Without further ceremony, one of the overseers, a tall, brawny man who Laura didn't recognise, began to use the sandal to spank the newcomer's bottom. The heavy sole slapped over and over again against Lucinda's beautifully rounded buttocks, rapidly turning her big, expansive bottom a blotchy shade of pink. The mistress wriggled her bum as it was smacked, in a manner which Laura instinctively knew would further excite the already hot-blooded group of men gathered around the whipping post. Sure enough, the sandal was soon dispensed with, the brawny overseer unable to resist the temptation to smack the provocatively writhing bottom with his hand, obviously delighting in the feeling of his skin against the smouldering flesh of his victim's bare bum-mounds.

His hand lingered after each smack, Laura noticed, feeling the mistress's bottom; his fingers nuzzled at the deep groove cleaving her bottom cheeks. And as the spanking continued, the brawny punisher became ever more bold, until he was blatantly groping the squirming captive's pink sex after each hot smack he delivered.

To a man, the overseers were eager to take their turn at beating the disproportionately large moons of Mistress Lucinda. Her bare buttocks squirmed beneath the cuts of both cane and riding crop, felt again the harsh, scolding slap of the sandal, and were spanked, squeezed and fondled by as many hands as the overseers possessed between them. In Laura's reckoning, by the time they brought to a close their devilish torture of the writhing, squealing and totally helpless blond, they had each taken their turn to feel her up, and many of the more lecherous had thrust their grubby fingers inside her, exploring the womanly softness of her vagina, while all the time mauling her big white breasts.

It was the whistle sounding which saved the mistress from further torment. The sweating brute who was groping her at the time pulled his fingers from within her and delivered a final hefty slap to her big pink bottom. Then she was untied and assisted to the gate of the field, where the large wooden wagon which had transported the women to the farmhouse at lunchtime was again waiting for them.

The women downed their tools and shuffled across to their transportation. Laura, in spite of the heat, and the sweat which sheathed her body, found herself involuntarily shivering as she thought about the scene she had just witnessed. It was clear to her that she, along with the other women, was at the mercy of a pack of animals; grim, savage men who would take their pleasure wherever and however they desired.

It was little consolation that the working day was at an end. Laura knew that, as long as she was a prisoner on the Farm, there could be no escape from the rod, and no escape either from the stinking brutes that oversaw her in the field.

It was a sobering thought, and one which stayed with her throughout the ordeal of dinner, as she sat with her shorts at her ankles, impaled on a wicked anal plug, sipping Gerda's vile green gruel.

After dinner, the workers from Field Three trudged back to the wagon and were transported out of the farmyard and along another dirt track. Mistress Lucinda kept very much to herself during the journey, pressing her face through the bars of the cage and no doubt, Laura thought, wishing she were back at the manor house, enjoying a platter of wild pheasant or whatever it was the landed gentry ate for their supper.

The other women obviously knew who she was, that much was evident from the smug looks and knowing smiles they passed between themselves. And Laura had thought her situation was bad! However disorientated she was, however aware of her position as the 'new girl', she did at least retain a certain anonymity. To her workmates, she was probably nothing other than the latest poor soul to find herself entrenched in the culture of the Farm.

But Lucinda was different.

What was she to the other women? The fiancée of the man responsible for keeping them captive; the woman who had shared his bed; the jodhpur-wearing horse rider who would occasionally trot her favourite white stallion past the three fields, watching impassively as various among the women were ruthlessly whipped by their overseers.

And Lucinda could expect no easy passage to be afforded her by the overseers either. The enthusiasm with which they'd beaten and mauled her in the field was proof enough of that. Clearly, they were as delighted as the women to have such exalted company among them, and would in no way be slow to take full advantage of the situation.

The wagon pulled up at a grim-looking concrete building. Windowless, and with a roof made of corrugated iron, it was long and low in shape, and Laura instinctively knew that they'd arrived at the dormitory of which Margaret had earlier spoken.

Without a word being uttered nor an instruction given, the women alighted from the wagon and trooped into the building through a narrow doorway, next to which an overseer stood menacingly rapping his cane against his leg. As Laura had expected, the building was indeed a dormitory, lined on either side with bunk beds that were made-up with the most rudimentary of flimsy coverings.

They filed into the room and walked to their beds. They began removing their work garments, neatly folding them and placing them on the floor at the bottom of the bunks. Laura and Lucinda stood in the doorway, uncertain of where to go.

"You two are there," an overseer gruffly informed them, indicating with his cane towards a spare bunk bed. The two newcomers moved swiftly across to their designated bunk and undressed as quickly as they could. Laura was somewhat perplexed by what her workmates had done after removing their clothing. Each woman had turned towards and taken hold of one of the bedposts at the bottom of their respective bunks.

Knowing better than to await an instruction to do so, the American imitated the position. She gripped the top of the right-hand bedpost with both hands and shifted her feet so that they were eight to ten inches away from its base, just as the other women had done. The posture caused her breasts to hang downwards and made her bottom more pronounced. She turned to her left and saw that, next to her, Lucinda had sensibly adopted the same pose against the opposite bedpost.

It was clear to Laura that, once again, she could expect something to be done to her bottom. As with all postures women on the Farm were commanded to strike, this new one achieved the aim of making her buttocks more vulnerable, ensuring that whatever devilish intention the overseers had would be implemented to maximum effect.

The sudden sound of a female voice made Laura turn her head towards the door. At the entrance to the building she could see the fearsome Gerda, cane in hand, light-heartedly sharing a joke with the overseer lurking in the doorway.

"Heads down, buttocks high!" growled one of the brutes who had accompanied them to their sleeping quarters. There was a sudden creaking of bedposts and shuffling of feet on the dormitory's tiled floor, the women ensuring they were positioned as instructed. Laura heard the sound of Gerda's high-heeled shoes clicking ominously against the polished floor as the German woman took four purposeful steps into the room.

The next sound the American heard was the familiar swishing of rattan through the air, followed by the sharp cracking noise made as a cane struck a bare bottom.

Another footstep; another swiping sound; another crack.

Another pair of buttocks disciplined.

Gerda efficiently made her way down one side of the

room, mercilessly administering a solitary cane-stroke to each pair of naked bottom-cheeks that she passed. Each woman, as she was caned, squealed or groaned or gurgled in pain, utterances of discomfort that were then swiftly drowned out by the sound of the wicked rattan landing on the next bare bottom in line.

Laura felt the butterflies fluttering in her stomach. Stroke after miserable stroke brought the grim German mistress ever nearer to her bunk.

Laura did as she'd been told and kept her head low, but as her sense of anxiety gathered, she couldn't resist a furtive sideways glance, bringing into her field of vision Lucinda's big hanging breasts and, beyond—ominously—the women at the next bunk, flinching and squealing as their bottoms were lashed.

So now the moment had come. The powerful German woman had reached her and Lucinda's bunk. Laura heard the sound of Gerda's high-heeled shoes clicking against the tiles, the big blond whip mistress moving herself into a suitable position from which to cane the next four wobbling orbs of female bum flesh.

Laura would hear one more cane stroke, she thought to herself, one more swish and crack as the rod landed on Lucinda's broad bottom; and then, the stroke after that she would not only hear, but feel as well, as it cut into the flesh of her own bare ass.

Well, that was what she thought, anyway.

Six hefty swipes of the cane later, Laura's bottom remained untouched. Lucinda was squealing and wailing next to her, and Laura could feel the whole bed frame shaking as the newly arrived Lucinda, still tightly clutching the bedpost, writhed frantically while Gerda's cane cruelly performed a tortuous dance across her aristocratic buttocks.

Ridiculous though it seemed, Laura was completely

unprepared when the vicious rod finally did crack into her naked bottom. She gasped and choked, and felt certain she was going to wet herself. She knew as well that her instinctive reaction to the cut had been to wiggle her ass provocatively. She hated herself for not having greater self-restraint. It stood to reason, after all, that the more sumptuous her bum seemed, the more likely she was to get it well-striped. And extra cuts, like the ones Lucinda had just taken, was the last thing she needed!

Yet still, there was that feeling of which she couldn't rid herself; that maybe, in truth, it was far from the last thing she needed; that actually, she had never been more excited, more stirred up emotionally, than as the throbbing pain of a cane stroke burned through her ass cheeks.

"Bed!" an overseer instructed, interrupting her meandering train of thought. The women moved briskly from their punishment positions, some clambering up the ladders that rested against the sides of the beds to the top bunks, others sliding into the lower beds. Gerda tapped Laura's bottom with her cane to get her attention and then indicated to the top mattress, and she wasted no time in climbing up the ladder and crawling under the rough blanket that had been provided for her warmth.

The lights went out the instant Gerda had left the room, bringing to an end the first traumatic day of Laura's new life on the Farm.

9

Her eyes, when they opened, were met by darkness. First, the natural darkness of nighttime in a windowless room; then, a different darkness altogether. Rough male hands dragged a hood over her head before she had time to react. As cords were tugged tight at the neck of the garment to secure it in place, other hands ripped away her blanket and clutched hold of her ankles, pulling them wide and tightly fastening them to the bedposts at the bottom of the bunk. Fingers tainted with the scent of nicotine snapped handcuffs to her wrists, drew her arms up above her head and manacled her to the headrest.

Laura knew better than to speak. Even in the few hours she'd been there, she'd realised that talking had no place on the Farm; so much so, in fact, that she was increasingly unable to make any kind of utterance at all, so quickly had she become familiar with her own silence.

She'd become familiar, as well, with the sound of Lucinda whimpering. It was a sound she heard again as she lay on her bunk, bound and spread-eagled.

"Up the ladder," came a murmured instruction, presumably from one of the men who'd so effectively immobilised Laura. The bed shook gently as the blond woman carried out the command, climbing up to the top bunk. Laura was kept informed of her bunkmate's progress by the sounds of her constant sniffling, and the high-pitched squeal she emitted as, inevitably, her bottom was given a hefty slap.

"Get between her legs, bitch-dog, on your knees."

The lower part of the mattress sank as Lucinda swung herself into the required position. It had been an ominous command which the overseer had given. Laura could only hope she was wrong about what would happen next.

"Get your face between her thighs and lick!"

It was another voice that spat the dreadful imperative. Laura heard herself yelp the word 'no!' and tried vainly to haul herself upright. Her progress was terminated by the sickening pain that coursed through her shoulder blades. Her sudden upwards movement had wrenched her bound arms almost from their sockets. Thwarted in her initial effort to protect herself, she tried desperately to bring her thighs together, twisting and turning on her rump in the hope of somehow concealing her sex. The attempt proved futile. Her legs had been pulled too far apart, fastened too tightly.

"Lick, bitch!" The angry command was followed by the touch of long soft hair against Laura's thighs as Lucinda's head was pushed towards her exposed genitalia. She heard a sudden slapping sound—rough palm spanking naked buttocks, she assumed—and Lucinda's hot choking breath against her sex.

"Eat her cunt!" an overseer demanded, and Laura felt the blond woman's face mashed into the soft flesh of her vagina. "No!" she moaned as Lucinda's tongue tentatively lapped against her sex, tickling the swollen hood of her clitoris. She bucked her body, thrusting her groin into the air in an attempt to avoid the licking she was being given.

The swift movement proved of no use. The flesh of her sex caught on Lucinda's tongue as she shifted upwards, stimulating her nerve endings and causing her skin to tingle madly. She was sickened to the pit of her stomach by what was happening to her—her legs stretched wide while another woman tongued her pussy; but there was no avoiding or denying the sensations, the delightful stabs of exquisite pleasure, that set her loins on fire.

She frantically contorted her body in a desperate attempt to avoid the forced attentions of the insistent tongue; hands rested against her abdomen and crushed her into the mattress, keeping her sex lips in position for the snivelling blond woman to lick and suck.

Laura murmured then, as she felt Lucinda's tongue slip into her vagina and tickle her inner flesh. There had been no instruction to do that, no terrible sound of a big heavy palm slapping against naked ass flesh, urging the action. So why had Lucinda done it? Why was she allowing her tongue to linger there, licking away at Laura's love-hole, sucking her juices?

Then the teasing tongue slid out and briefly tickled Laura's vulva again, before breaking off from its feverish toil to be replaced by teeth that nibbled away at her exposed and swollen clitoris.

Her face masked to a terrible blackness by the heavy hood, Laura could find no easy distraction from the delicious sensations between her thighs. Lucinda was working with a disconcerting frenzy, nibbling and chewing at her clitoris, licking and sucking at the tender flesh of her pussy, lapping at the juices that Laura knew were gathering there. She wanted to explode; to buck and thrust until she was clutched by the orgasm she sensed lingered only moments away. Yet she wanted to weep as well, as she felt the soft strands of Lucinda's hair stroke her legs and the avid stab of her tongue as it was once again buried within her love pot.

She hated what was happening to her. In spite of the heat, the lust it was generating between her thighs, she hated it. And she hated Lucinda too, for the way she was enthusiastically licking her out, revelling in obviously lesbian tendencies.

Laura heard a squeal, and no longer felt the hair against her thighs, the tongue within her cunt. Instead, she felt hands at her ankle straps, untying her. She squealed herself then, from beneath her hood, as her legs were drawn up above her and refastened at the bedhead, either side of her handcuffed wrists. Her knees pressed against her breasts and Laura felt her heart pounding anxiously within her chest. What next, she wondered. What fiendish plan did her nighttime visitors have for her now?

She heard another heavy slap, followed immediately by a girlish shriek. Next came the gruff voice which had instructed Lucinda to bury her face in Laura's sex.

"Now her arse," it said.

Soft feminine hands rested against the Laura's buttocks. She felt Lucinda's thumbs press against the flesh to either side of her anus and gently ease open the secret orifice. Her skin crawled as, for the first time in her life, a tongue slid across her bottom-hole, methodically licking at the ring of exposed and sensitive flesh. The tongue danced back and forth over the hole, lightly tickling the surrounding skin, teasingly flicking at the flaps of wrinkled flesh adorning the tight aperture.

"Oh no!" Laura moaned. Realisation of her full shame, her sheer degradation, flooded her mind. She couldn't help but be aware of the eagerness with which Lucinda's tongue was bathing her asshole, seeking to titillate every puckered nook, every crinkled cranny of her tight little butt-opening. She gurgled, grimaced, and tried futilely to twist away as Lucinda shifted her weight, gained greater leverage and eased Laura's upturned bottom-cheeks further apart. Instinctively, the American suspected what was coming, and almost immediately was proved right. Her hooded face flushed a burning red as she felt Lucinda's tongue slide up her asshole.

Lucinda's hair brushed against the backs of her victim's thighs as her head bobbed up and down, her stiff tongue rhythmically thrusting in and out of Laura's gently yielding back passage.

Laura couldn't help but gasp as the terrible experience

continued. Tears tumbled from her eyes. Her occasional muffled sobs drew barely suppressed laughter from the onlooking overseers.

The shame of her position was almost too much to bear: laid wide open, her cunt no doubt glistening with a frothy blend of saliva and her own natural womanly juices, her brown bumhole thrust towards the ceiling, eagerly being fucked by another woman's tongue.

Lucinda thrust and wiggled her tongue with wild abandon, reaching further up inside Laura's rectum than the American could ever have imagined possible.

When the blonde was finally wrenched away from the drenched orifice and manhandled from the bed, it was to allow the overseers to unfasten Laura from her shameful position, flip her over onto her stomach and refasten her, binding her ankles to the lower bedposts and her wrists to the bedhead once more.

Almost as soon as she'd been secured, Laura felt a terrible stinging sensation in her buttocks. For just an instant, the tortuous instrument that had inflicted the pain rested across her bare bottom. Then it was gone, only to return a moment later—accompanied by a crisp and terrible cracking sound—to burn her bumflesh mere millimetres below where the initial stroke had hit.

She buried her head in her pillow and gritted her teeth. The strap—or whatever it was—rained blow after savage blow against her buttocks until she was lewdly jiggling her naked bottom in a frenzied, feverish display of pain.

Rough hands clutched her smouldering rump flesh, and the bed creaked loudly as an unknown party clambered aboard. Laura smelt the scent of sweet cider, felt hot, panting breath against the nape of her neck, and almost had her own breath crushed from her as a heavy frame lowered itself against her sweat-drenched back.

She gasped then as hairy knees pushed against her

spread-eagled legs, forcing them wider still. Briefly, Laura felt the thick stem of her assailant's sex muscle nuzzling against her sopping wet cunt lips, then held her breath as he pushed inside her. Fingers clutched her black hair, the brute's rough tongue slaked a rugged path across her neck, and the thick cock within her slippery vagina throbbed and thrusted, roughly pounding into the saliva-soaked channel with such force that Laura felt sure it would rip her wide open.

The beast fucked her for several minutes, pistoning in and out of her with strokes so powerful that her head was repeatedly slammed against the metal bar to which her wrists had been manacled.

With a snort, he withdrew, his gnarled fingers instantly digging into Laura's buttocks and wrenching them apart.

"Please, no!" she begged as she felt the warm night air circulating in her bottom-cleft. She grimaced as the overseer stretched her bottom-cheeks as wide open as he could manage, and pleaded with him again when she felt the bulbous head of his cock press against her slithery anus.

She was plundered in her back passage then.

The thick muscle tore through her ring of resistant anal flesh, and ploughed deep inside her most shameful place. The brutish overseer sank on top of her stretched, perspiring body once she'd been comprehensively impaled, and moved his fleshy hips up and down in a fast and merciless rhythm. Laura gripped the bed's headrest tightly and tried desperately, pointlessly, to blank her mind.

Her best efforts yielded no return whatsoever. There was no escape; no way to rid herself of the pain, the humiliation, the awful, soul-destroying degradation, of having a man take his pleasure inside her bottom. Flat on her stomach, legs fastened wide apart, a stiff cock bunging her ass-crack; Laura's experiences on the Farm had reached a new and miserable level of torment.

She was aware of nothing except her bottom—her smarting buttocks and her sore and burning rectum—and the grotesque shaft that squirmed and pumped within it. The rigid muscle pistoned in and out of her anus, applying hard, vigorous strokes that seemed only to terminate once deep within her bowel.

Her bum had never been penetrated by a cock before—the anal plug she'd been made to sit on at lunch and suppertime aside—and her eyes watered from the strangely exquisite pain. She hoped against hope for a merciful unconsciousness to claim her.

The overseer's unwieldy monster continued to throb and rage inside her tight bottom-mouth. Laura found herself stretching her legs as far apart as she possibly could, desperately trying to widen her anus, to relieve the tear jerking discomfort she was suffering deep within her bottom.

It was a long and languid sigh of sheer relief which Laura exhaled when, finally, having resorted to flexing her sphincter muscles as tightly as she could in a desperate effort to milk the grizzled overseer, he gave out a low groan and released his hot jets of fluid deep into her battered anus.

She felt the still-pumping monstrosity slide from her bumhole. Fingers were at her buttocks almost immediately, holding them apart. She felt something else then, something which she could only imagine to be some kind of anal plug, being slipped into place.

It was only as, finally, her bottom cheeks were released and her ankles unfastened, that she became consciously of the sounds which had been emanating from Lucinda's bed. The bunk, which had groaned and creaked noisily while Laura was being used, continued to shift rhythmically. Laura could hear Lucinda moaning softly, an occasional sob catching in the blond woman's throat, and knew that her bunkmate was enduring an ordeal similar to her own.

The hood was untied and dragged roughly from her head. It took a few moments for her eyes to readjust themselves to the natural darkness. Once they'd done so, Laura was able to see from her vantage point, sprawled on the top bunk, a gruesome overseer crouching at the side of Lucinda's bed, thrusting his groin forward time and time again. Laura couldn't see Lucinda from where she lay, but realised from the assailant's position that he must have had her pinned over the edge of the bed and was thrusting into her from behind.

Laura wondered which hole he was using and caught herself, rather ungenerously, hoping the blond pussy-sucking bitch was getting it hard in the ass!

She saw the overseer's body stiffen, heard him groan, and knew that the moment had come. Once satiated, he pulled himself clear of his sobbing mount and stood up; then he and his friend—presumably the brute who had used Laura—hauled Lucinda up onto her bed and swiftly made their exit.

Welcome to the Farm!

She could hear Lucinda whimpering quietly on the bed below, but resisted the urge to try and comfort her. After all, it wasn't as if she didn't have enough to sob about herself; why should she waste time comforting the big-bottomed newcomer, especially after the relish with which the blond had worked Laura's cunt and asshole over with her tongue?

Laura found herself wondering how many other among the women had the same tendencies. She resolved to remain vigilant, alert to the possibility of danger coming from unexpected sources. Not that there would be much she could do, in the event, to save herself; if the overseers decided that some frigging lesbian should eat her out, she'd no doubt be made powerless to resist.

She tested the handcuffs that still bound her wrists to the headrest. There was absolutely no possibility of escape. So she resolved to make herself comfortable instead—as comfortable as she could with her wrists manacled above her and an anal plug wedged in her cum-flooded rectum—and do her best to get some much-needed sleep.

10

Morning. It was Hans's heavy footsteps against the tiled floor of the dormitory that woke Laura. Almost before she'd had time to open her eyes properly, one of the overseers had unfastened her handcuffs. As she rubbed her wrists, he plied her buttocks apart and she felt the anal plug being removed, pulled from within the confines of her bottom by the short cord to which it was attached. No words were spoken, no instructions given.

Released from her bondage, Laura took her lead from the other women, all of whom had swiftly got themselves up from bed and reassumed the punishment position against the bedposts.

Hans made his way along one side of the dormitory and back up the other, doing as Gerda had done the night before—using a whippy cane to apply one fearful lash to each pair of beautifully presented bare buttocks that he passed.

The women dressed then, putting on the fresh clothing—sleeveless shirt and shorts, of course—that had been left for them at the bottom of their beds.

Laura avoided eye contact with Lucinda; it was more than she could manage to in any way acknowledge the woman who, only hours earlier, had buried her tongue in her pussy and bumhole. Yet, in spite of herself, in spite of the feelings of contempt and loathing which she harboured for her, Laura couldn't help but feel strangely close to the blond woman, as if a bond, some form of inexplicable link, existed between them as a result of the traumas they had shared during the dark hours of the night.

The women made their way then out of the dormitory, taking a route around the back of the grim building into an open yard that had been concealed from Laura's view when she'd arrived the previous evening. Gerda was there, as were a number of the overseers who had presided over the women in Field Three the day before. To the far side of the dusty yard stood three ramshackle wooden cubicles, lined up side by side. Within each of the rudimentary constructions, all of which had two sides and a back but was open to view, a toilet was fitted.

The women shuffled into three distinct lines, one queue in front of each cubicle. Laura joined the line behind Margaret, who smiled furtively at her.

"I know what happened in the night," she whispered. "It was dreadful."

"I'm not so sure the other new girl thought so," the American whispered back, her eyes fixing on Lucinda, who stood a little way ahead of them in the far queue.

"The best thing you can do is forget all about it. You need to concentrate on today, and make sure you carry on keeping your head down."

Sound advice, but forgetting the traumas of the night would be easier said than done. And as for keeping her head down, that was exactly what she thought she'd done the previous day, so how come she'd had the early hours' visitation?

Her thought processes were interrupted by a barked command from Hans.

"First three girls to the pans," he instructed. The girls at the front of the queues made their way forward, entering their respective cubicles and turning round a hundred-and-eighty degrees so that they had the toilets behind them and were facing their fellow workers.

"Present and sit!" Hans growled. In perfect unison, each of the three women tugged their pants down their legs and lowered their bottoms onto the toilet seats. The big German wandered across the yard in front of the three cubicles, glancing in to each to ensure they had followed his instructions. As he sauntered, he rapped his length of cane purposefully against his knee-high boot, an ominous warning to them of what they could expect if they disobeyed.

Gerda stood at the side of the cubicles with a clipboard and pen, her own cane tucked neatly beneath her arm. Laura watched as Hans caught his sister's eye, and she returned his glance with an accompanying nod; confirmation, Laura thought, that she was ready for whatever was going to happen next.

Laura's mind was whirling. As with everything she had witnessed on the Farm, this latest development intrigued her greatly, in spite of the terrible trepidation that was also growing within her.

Her eyes followed the pacing figure of Hans and occasionally flitted towards the cubicles. The three women cut ridiculous, miserable figures, seated on their toilets, shorts twisted around their ankles.

"Prepare yourselves, ladies," Hans advised. He ceased his monotonous striding, and turned to face the cubicles.

"One, two, three—strain!"

Laura switched her attention from the powerful, cane-wielding figure of the German overseer to the three huddled women in the cubicles. The command obviously had the same effect and held the same weight as the instruction to 'present', judging by the swiftness with which the seated women complied. Muscles tensing, their faces contorted masks of concentration, each of them pushed hard, desperately trying to deposit something into their toilet pan.

"And stop." The women's faces reflected their relief. Their muscles relaxed and they exhaled long and languorous breaths. The woman in the left-hand cubicle was slower to respond than her companions, her tardiness pointed out by the watchful Gerda. Hans stormed into the cubicle, snatching at the woman's hair and dragging her from the toilet. He deposited her on the floor in front of the pan, and forced her face down into the dirt so that her bottom was the highest area of her body. Laura winced as the German powerhouse lashed the woman's buttocks with his cane.

"Do not continue to shit when you have been told to stop!" he growled. "Now back on the toilet seat and await your instructions!" He wrenched at her hair, guiding her back into her seated position.

"One, two, three—strain!" he barked again, and the women renewed their attempts to defecate.

"Stop!" Hans said at length. "Shorts off and hose your asses!"

The three women kicked off their pants, picked them up and made their way to a crumbling brick wall to the side of the cubicles. Each took hold of one of three hoses, all of which were lying on the ground, gently spewing water, and set about cleansing their bottoms. As they did so, the long-striding Gerda made her way from cubicle to cubicle, inspecting the contents of each toilet and scribbling notes on her clipboard.

"What happens if you don't come up with the goods?" Laura whispered to Margaret.

"Nothing. Gerda keeps a record of each woman's motions and assesses what's required in each individual case."

"What d'you mean?"

"She may decide after a few days that you need a high fibre diet, or in more extreme cases arrange for you to be given an enema."

Laura felt her heart sink. Was there any form of degradation not practised on the Farm? The last few hours had been her most traumatic yet, the early morning toilet ritual promising to introduce her to new levels of misery and distress. So you weren't even allowed to shit in private! Laura wondered why the overseers didn't just herd the women into pens, make them eat out of troughs and be done with it. They were being treated like animals; they might just as well be made to live like them as well.

As Laura continued with her anxiety-ridden musings, another three bottoms came to rest on the porcelain seats and strained to the sound of Hans's voice. The following three women included Lucinda, whose broad bottom bloomed across the whole expanse of toilet seat.

Again the German barked the instruction to 'strain'. Laura felt her heart pounding heavily in her chest as the dreadful Gerda drew her brother's attention to Lucinda.

"She is feigning, Hans," the stern looking mistress advised, "pretending to be straining when actually she is just sitting on her fat bottom looking smug."

Laura could tell from the expression on her face that Lucinda was becoming increasingly agitated during Hans and Gerda's brief discussion. As a new arrival herself, unable to accept the concept of evacuating her bowels on command and in front of a gathering of onlookers, Laura was well able to believe that Lucinda had been feigning her efforts. It was something which she herself might instinctively have tried, pointless though it was to do so, in an ill-judged attempt to save herself from the shame of defecating while people watched.

When she witnessed the consequence of Lucinda's foolish action, Laura's blood ran cold. Hans grasped Lucinda by the hair and dragged her out of the cubicle and across the yard to a wooden trestle. Two burly overseers assisted their commander in fastening her into position. Her ankles were tied to the trestles that rested at either end of the horizontal beam over which she was bent, securing her legs apart. Her wrists were bound to the legs of the trestle on the far side of the beam.

Lucinda squirmed against her bonds, desperately attempting to escape from the position which had so perfectly presented her large bottom for the cruel attentions of the muscular Hans. She received a terrible caning then, Hans bringing his wicked rattan whistling through the air time after time, whipping the flesh of her trembling bottom until it was a mass of livid weals.

Lucinda was quickly untied and dragged back across the yard to her cubicle. The overseers unceremoniously bundled her onto the toilet, cruelly squashing her bottom down into the pan, trapping her.

"Now shit, you little bitch!" snapped Gerda, swinging her cane through the air as a warning. The severe German mistress strode into the cubicle, the gloved left hand in which she held the rattan darting forward and clasping at a clump of the seated woman's long blond hair. Gerda steered Lucinda's head upward, exposing her tear-stained face, and proceeded to firmly slap her cheeks, delivering three hard blows to each side of her victim's face. She tugged her up then, still holding her hair, and bent her double against her own hip, before inspecting the toilet bowl.

"Nothing!" the German woman bellowed. "Nothing, you little minx!" She took hold of the cane in her right hand and steadying the sobbing Lucinda against her side, she began to lash angrily at the woman's big buttocks.

"You will learn a hard lesson, then," Gerda growled as she flogged the wobbling bottom-cheeks presented before her. "You will learn to strain when you are told to do so, and you will never again leave a toilet bowl empty."

After twelve fearsome strokes, during which the writhing, wailing Lucinda had descended to her knees and Gerda, driven by rage, had lashed at the jiggling buttocks in whatever position they'd happened to be presented to her, the terrible beating came to an end. Lucinda slumped facedown to the ground, revealing to the onlooking women the twin hillocks of her bottom, scowling a savage crimson in the early morning sunlight.

"Take the miserable bitch to the farmhouse," said Gerda, addressing the two brutes who had moments earlier reseated her on the toilet, "I will deal with her there. Next!"

"Next three girls to the pans!" barked Hans, echoing his sister's instruction. Three more women moved smartly forward, depositing their pants and seating themselves on the toilets. Their business finished, they removed their shorts, trotted to the hoses and washed their bottoms.

And so the early morning ritual continued. Laura watched Margaret strain, trot and wash before, on Hans's instruction, she finally made her own way to her designated cubicle, dropping her shorts and sitting down on the toilet. Bizarre though it was, she found herself feeling almost thankful she'd been fucked in the ass only a few hours earlier. The traumatised state of her sphincter muscle and the effect of having had two testicles-worth of cum pumped into her back passage ensured she gave the grim-looking Gerda more than enough about which to scribble notes on her clipboard.

The terrible routine of Laura's life continued for many sweltering days. Her mornings always began the same, with a ritual cane stroke delivered to each of the trembling workers as they stood at the bottom of their bunk beds, posteriors thrust outward, as though enthusiastic for the kiss of the rattan.

Then there was the toilet ritual. Occasionally, a number of the women would be ordered onto a small horse-driven cart and transported to the farmhouse. Margaret told the

American that they were being taken there to have enemas administered to them, a sign that Gerda was unhappy with the regularity of their bowel movement.

Laura determined to avoid the excruciating shame of that particular ordeal, and lay awake at night, in spite of her exhaustion, desperately attempting to strain her way to the threshold of a bowel movement in readiness for the morning routine.

Her desire to avoid one of Gerda's gruesome enemas was heightened by the reappearance of those who'd endured a treatment in the farmhouse. The unfortunate woman, or women, would be deposited in Field Three, in preparation for a day of hard labour, wearing the most ridiculous attire Laura had ever seen. In place of the regulation shorts, they would be wearing what she thought of as oversized padded diapers. These were kept in place all day, except of course, when the women were made to present their bottoms to be thrashed.

Laura became used to the sound of whistling canes and crops, and the sight of soft female bum flesh being turned crimson. During the course of the days which followed, she would occasionally experience, either at first hand or otherwise, some dreadful new punishment; some diabolical new torture which would serve to increase her feelings of helplessness and, perversely, her sense of simmering excitement.

The whipping post to which Lucinda had been bound when she'd first arrived in Field Three was occasionally put to good use. One young woman was fastened into position and laid bare from her shoulders to her ankles, after which she was whipped soundly across her back and buttocks. Another was taken across the thighs of an overseer as he sat on a fat sack of grain. He roughly peeled her pants down her legs and applied a riding crop to her buttocks, before using the heavy, dust-encrusted palm of his hand on her trembling cheeks, as though she were a naughty child.

Laura, too, found herself subjected to a different kind of punishment from that which was most familiarly administered in the field. Her overseer, having growled at her throughout the morning to dig faster, finally lost patience with the painstaking, one-paced manner in which she was upturning shovelfuls of earth.

"That's it," he snapped, "you're for it now!" and Laura prepared herself for the barked command to 'present!' Instead, she was grappled to the ground by the perspiring brute, and divested of her shorts. Flat out on her back, the midday sun burning down on her sweat-drenched face and stomach, her legs were clamped together and lifted up into the air. The overseer, crouching low, his arm encircling her legs to hold them high, then proceeded to smack her exposed buttocks with downward strokes of his riding crop, cracking the evil length of leather against first her right, then her left bum cheek until he had satisfactorily heated the full expanse of her posteriors.

Margaret, similarly, received regular beatings. On one occasion she even merited a trip to the whipping post when she accidentally dropped her shovel. Her shorts were pulled down and her bottom roundly smacked with the sole of a sandal; a form of punishment which, to Laura's mind, seemed agreeably mild by comparison with the cut of the cane or the swipe of the crop. The unexpected sound of the determinedly courageous Margaret beginning to squeal and beg for leniency quickly made Laura reassess her viewpoint, however.

Laura lost count of the number of days she had been at the Farm. Fatigued by the interminable hours spent labouring in the field, burned by the blistering sun and the scolding implements of torture wielded by the overseers, anxious about the early morning toilet ordeal, she had ceased to think in terms of time. Her day was measured not in hours and minutes but in strokes and lashes.

As she lay face down on her bed, her lower back too sunburnt, her buttocks too sore to allow her to adopt any other position, she drifted in and out of sleep. Drained of all energy, she was nevertheless unable to achieve anything more than the shallowest of sleeps. She was too anxious, always too anxious, about the morning toilet routine. Even as her body was enveloped by the comforting blanket of unconsciousness, her mind drove her back into a state of agitated wakefulness, urging her to continue with her night-time regime; the regular flexing, the tensing of her buttock muscles, exercising her sphincter, ensuring she was ready to 'deliver' when the order came to drop her shorts and sit on the toilet.

The feeling of a hand against her wrist startled her properly awake. Her mind, sluggish as she'd fought against the overwhelming desire to sleep, responded to the touch with admirable and unexpected speed, wondering if the terrible ordeal of her first night was about to be repeated.

As she felt a soft leather collar being fastened around her neck, and recalled that dreadful early experience, she instinctively tensed her buttock muscles— desperately, pointlessly attempting to offer some form of resistance against any attempted penetration of her bottom.

No attempt was made.

"You will come with me." The voice was young and distinctly lacking in authority.

A gentle tug on her neck collar urged Laura up onto her knees. Another gentle tug encouraged her towards the edge of her bed. Slowly, she shifted across the mattress and tentatively made her way down the stepladders from her bunk. Safely landed, she strained her eyes in an effort to identify her visitor. As she was led into the aisle that separated the two rows of dormitory beds, Laura caught her breath in horror. The stark bulb which glowered moodily in the small guardroom beyond the dormitory was shedding its dissolute light through the half open doorway. It was just enough to make out the pockmarked skin, the thick-framed glasses and the lank, tangled hair of the youth she had first encountered the day she had been brought to the Farm.

Laura had wondered who he was. One moment he'd been standing at Hans's side in the village inn, inspecting Laura's bare, upturned bum, the next he'd disappeared without trace, and she hadn't seen him since. Now he was taking her from the dormitory in the middle of the night, as though she were a dog on a lead. He gently made his way on tiptoe passed the rows of naked, slumbering women and out into the guardroom, where a fat overseer snored and gurgled. Laura followed behind him, her heart pounding in her chest, her breathing shallow and laboured, her body naked and trembling.

Where was he taking her? What should she do? It was a ludicrous situation in which she found herself. The youth had obviously crept in while the overseer slept, and was smuggling Laura out of the dormitory for reasons only he could possible know. She wondered about alerting the sleeping guard to her imminent kidnap, but somehow couldn't bring herself to do so. After all, why should she alert the overseer, one of the brutes who took such pleasure in beating her? What advantage would she gain from that? He would only stop the oily-faced youth in his tracks and then return Laura to her bed to await her next thrashing. It was hardly an appealing option!

Yet she was disgusted by the vile youth, and had hated every spine-tingling moment she'd had to endure on that first dreadful day, when his bespectacled eyes were boring into her flesh, drinking in every detail of her shamefully exposed bottom, humiliating her to her very soul.

With another gentle tug, the youth guided her out of the building and into the open air, and, suddenly, Laura knew that there was no longer a choice to be made. She winced as sharp twigs and stones dug into her bare feet, and stumbled in the oily youth's wake, her heart beginning to hammer like a piston in her chest as she realised where he was leading her.

He was taking her into the woods!

11

Gritting her teeth and grimacing as her skin was lashed by spiky thorns and brambles, Laura staggered through the woodland, pulled at an energetic pace by the lank-haired adolescent towards an unknown fate.

After what seemed to be an interminable period of suffering, being scratched and cut by branches, nettles and briars, she emerged into a small brightly moonlit clearing.

The youth had brought them to their intended destination.

Laura felt terribly exposed by the moonlight, and, foolish though it seemed given the hopelessness of her situation, found herself attempting to conceal her breasts and bush of pubic hair from the lustful eyes of her bespectacled young captor.

"Hands on your head," he snapped, quite obviously irritated by her ridiculous attempt to hide her charms.

"What are you going to do with me?" Laura questioned, her words catching slightly in her throat, so unused had she become to the act of speaking. It was strange to be standing there, stripped naked in front of an ugly pimple-laden adolescent; and peculiar as well to feel that for once, perhaps, she had room for manoeuvre; an opportunity to bargain.

Laura didn't really know why she felt that. After all, there she was, standing nude in a moonlit clearing, her hands on her head and a leash around her neck—how could she possibly feel in any way empowered? And yet, there was something; something about the uncertainty in her captor's voice that had served to remind her of how young he was, how inexperienced, maybe even naive.

"I'm going to do with you whatever I want," the

bespectacled teenager announced.

"What's your name, honey?" she enquired.

"That's none of your business."

Laura could detect the slightest of German accents in the youth's voice. It was nowhere near as distinctive as that of Hans or Gerda, but it was noticeable nonetheless. It seemed fair to assume he was in some way related to Hans and his sister.

"I saw you the other day with Hans, didn't I? Is he a friend of yours?"

"My brother, if you must know."

"And are you just like your big brother, honey?"

"Like him?"

"Yeah, do you like the same things?"

The adolescent seemed confused by Laura's line of questioning. His brows knitted together quizzically beneath the soft caress of the moonlight.

"I don't understand."

The merest hint of a smile played at the corners of Laura's mouth. Teasingly, she batted her long dark eyelashes at the strange young man. "I mean, do you want to smack my bum, just like your big brother does?"

The youth shuffled uncomfortably. Laura could tell that he was becoming increasingly aroused by her playful seduction.

Then…

"Present!" he snapped suddenly. His unexpected resort to the familiar command caught Laura off her guard. She hesitated for a second. Barked by a snarling overseer, the instruction carried all the weight required to make the American immediately reach for her ankles. When uttered by an acne-ridden youth, the issue wasn't so clear. Who was he, this spot-infested creature? Why should she adopt the humiliating pose at his behest? But what if she didn't? He was after all, Hans's little brother—

there was no knowing what trouble she might be buying herself if she disobeyed. So she did what came naturally, performing what had become an almost reflex action for her and clasping her ankles.

Almost as soon as she'd adopted the position, she began to rebuke herself. Silly frigging bitch, she thought, you've conceded your advantage; you had the little bastard off-guard. Now look at you; hands at your ankles and moons in the moonlight! The spotty nerd's got you now!

Better make an attempt to regain control.

"What would you do if I tried to run away, honey?" she questioned. Laura was looking up from her doubled-over position, her eyes following the boy's movements as he shuffled through the thick wet grass, searching for something.

"I would raise the alarm, and tell the overseer on duty that you had escaped. I would cut myself open with my switchblade and claim that, when I had tried to stop you, you had wounded me. You would be captured and the skin beaten off your body."

Laura concluded her decision to 'present' had been the right one. The little shit had got it all worked out. Sure, he wasn't supposed to have snuck into the dormitory and kidnapped her; sure, there was a possibility that the overseer, and Hans, and Gerda, and Uncle Tom Cobbly for that matter, would be suspicious of his story; but the fact remained, the pimplehead was Hans and Gerda's family.

She, on the other hand, was a prisoner of the Farm, and dreaded the very thought of what they'd do to her ass if the four-eyed brat span his yarn.

So she clenched her teeth together and was thankful for small mercies, such as the fact that, in the moonlight, the teenager wouldn't be able to see that she was becoming red-faced with the shame of it all; and the fact that there was nobody else there to see her being humiliated by an ugly, greasy-faced adolescent.

Then she saw the youth stoop and pick up a long length of thick cane. She found herself wishing to God the implement could have been as small as the mercies she was busy being thankful for.

"Hey!" she murmured. "Listen, honey, is there anything at all I can do to stop you using that thing on me?"

The pimply-faced cane-wielder experimentally swung his rattan through the air. The terrible slicing noise made Laura's heart skip a beat.

"I get enough cane during the daytime, honey," she continued as the youth approached. "Can't we do something more... more pleasurable during the night-time?" Laura hated herself for what she was saying. She wasn't quite sure whether her stomach was churning with fear of a beating or with disgust at the prospect of pleasuring the lank-haired teenager. Nonetheless, she continued with her strategy, reminding herself that her priority was to save her miserable ass from another thrashing. "I'd like to do something nice to you, honey," she implored. "Why don't you put that big ol' cane down and let me do something nice to you?"

The youth had stopped in his tracks, hesitant, uncertain of himself, obviously intrigued by her suggestion. It was a sure sign that, just as Laura's intuition had told her, there was indeed room for manoeuvre.

"Can I, honey?" she asked in her most pleading voice. "Can I do something nice to you?"

The youth remained silent for a moment, after which he gently nodded his head, yes.

Laura stood up, excited by the minor victory she seemed to have achieved. Even so, the sense of relief that coursed through her at having successfully side-stepped the caning was prematurely terminated by a sudden rising of bile into her throat, her mind dwelling too closely on the distasteful prospect she had embraced in its stead. She would have to pull out all the stops, she knew that, and the very thought made her feel sick.

She forced her mouth to curl upwards into a smile and sidled over to the unpleasant youth, pressed her breasts and groin against his gently trembling body, and planted a luscious kiss on his dry, flaky lips. Her hands slid purposefully down to his corduroy trousers as her tongue teasingly nuzzled into his mouth. Expertly, she began to unfasten his belt and zipper.

"What's you name, honey?" she whispered into his ear, tenderly kissing his neck.

"Peter," he whispered, with barely contained excitement.

"That's a real nice name, Peter." Laura's fingers slithered inside his trousers and slipped into his shorts, searching for his manhood. She found the muscle to be surprisingly thick, and caressed it with the lightest of touches as it twitched and bulged, seeping slimy fluid against the already-dampened material of his underpants.

Her long fingernails teased his scrotum bag, gently scratching at the hairy skin drawn tight as a drum around his swollen testicles. She ceasing her expert caress of his genitals momentarily, and planted another succulent kiss against his lips, at the same time firmly tugging his trousers and shorts down to his thighs. In one fluid movement she pulled her tongue from his mouth and dropped to her knees on the soft grass. Her fingers reassumed control of Peter's manhood, taking firm but gentle hold of the pulsating beast around its base while her tongue began to tickle away at the tiny, weeping eyelet.

She was relieved to find that, in spite of her worst fears, the gruesome Peter kept himself perfectly fresh and clean. Her concerns allayed, she determined to perform the task with her usual relish. She drew him into her mouth, fanning the skin with her hot breath, and began to suck enthusiastically. She used her tongue to lick the flesh of his foreskin, and occasionally tickled at the still-dribbling glans.

All the while, her fingers gently scratched across the skin of his scrotum, every now and then delicately squeezing one or other of his tightened cum-heavy testicles. Her head bobbed back and forth as she sucked avidly, engulfing the whole length of his shaft with her lips and mouth—until the monstrous glans nuzzled the back of her throat—and then pulling virtually clear of it, only to thrust forward at the last moment and once again consume the throbbing muscle.

The sucking continued in perfect rhythm with the increasingly feverish moans of the pockmarked adolescent. Laura decided it was in her best interests to draw his sting completely. She would make him cum in her mouth and would swallow the repellent seed down into her stomach. She remembered only too clearly the strapping Sally had endured from John Templeton when she had failed to swallow his deposit. Laura was determined to complete the job, and remove any possible excuse the youth might have found to beat her.

It was then, as she determined on her course of action, that the plan went dreadfully awry. Without warning, she felt the youth's fingers clasp chunks of her thick hair and found herself being savagely pulled away from her task. The force with which Peter had torn her clear of his cock sent Laura tumbling backwards into the wet grass, bemused by her captor's sudden mood swing.

"Present!" he growled, stumbling forward, his legs

caught up in the tangle of twisted garments at his ankles. He stooped and picked up the cane, aiming a gentle swipe at Laura's hip, as she lay stunned in the thick grass.

"But I thought we agreed!" she protested. Her mind reeled, realising that she'd been duped by the adolescent.

"I wish to beat you now," growled Peter, as though offering some form of explanation, "Present!"

Laura scrambled to her feet, her skin soaked from the wetness of the grass. She bent herself double, clasped her ankles and inwardly cursed the spotty little shit. How stupid had she been, Laura thought to herself! How could she have imagined, even for a moment, that she could trade-off with the oily youth? He had her naked in a wood late at night, a length of thick cane in his hand! If she offered him a blowjob, sure the pimply run was going to accept it—but there was no way he was going to miss out on using that frigging cane!

In her doubled-over posture, Laura watched the youth take up a position behind her and to her side, and carefully measure his distance from her ideally presented bottom. His trousers were still at his ankles.

He began to flog her then, swinging the fat, heavy cane through the sultry night air time and time again, bringing it cracking down with all the force he could muster against her dew-sodden bottom. Tears first trickled and then poured from Laura's eyes as her buttocks caught fire.

Stroke after vicious stroke tore into her flesh, sending shock waves of fierce pain lancing through her upturned bumcheeks. The vicious caning continued until the savage Peter was gasping for breath. The power of the strokes caused Laura to stumble forward and stagger in the tangle of long grass at her feet. She tried to regain her balance, tried desperately to reassume the required position in readiness for the next stroke.

Heaving from his exertions, the youth finally hurled the cane aside. Although too traumatised by the whipping to have kept a count, Laura was certain her captor had lashed some two-dozen or more strokes across her quivering bottom-cheeks. It was the cruellest, the most merciless whipping she had taken; a clandestine flogging, administered to her by a greasy adolescent who knew it might be the only chance he ever got to flog her.

Nobody knew about it and nobody would tell, so she had been completely at his mercy. He had shown her none.

Laura saw the youth sink to his knees in the grass behind her, and wondered what devilment he would perpetrate next. His hands grasped her scorched buttocks, pulling them apart. Unceremoniously, he buried his tongue into her anus.

"No," she sobbed, as he set about licking and sucking her most secret place. Laura hated being licked there. Not the sensation itself, a teasing tickle inside the mouth of her bottom that was almost pleasurable, but the dreadful feeling of shame which the action induced within her.

Somebody else's tongue buried inside her clammy ass! How did she taste? What if she tasted bad?

It was foolish, ridiculous, to give a damn about how the insides of her ass tasted, she knew that. It was the lecherous youth's decision to eat her bumhole out, after all; why should she care how she tasted? Why should she care if he was sampling her shit?

But as he plunged into the depths of her anus, his tongue poking away like a miniature penis, Laura knew that her sense of shame was derived from something more than the irrational, almost 'polite' concern that the dank confines of her bum may not have been a pleasant taste experience.

No, her sense of shame came from the fact that another person should ever actually find out how she tasted there, should ever have the opportunity to strip her so flagrantly, so comprehensively, of her privacy, of what was probably her most intimate secret.

She knew as well that the bespectacled adolescent was inevitably reaming her shithole for a reason. It was that knowledge which weighed most heavily on her.

The youth didn't lick her for long. Slipping his tongue from the tight confines of her anus, he hauled himself to his feet and nuzzled his wet cock into her exposed bum cleft.

"What am I going to do now?" he asked her. Laura felt her stomach churn. She knew only too well what was coming next—and realised as well, from Peter's suddenly firm tone, that he had found a fresh resolve, a new confidence that boded no good for her.

She clasped her ankles more tightly, mashed her teeth together and determinedly murmured the response that she knew was required.

"You're going to fuck me in the ass."

"Do you want to be fucked in the ass?"

There was no point resisting the inevitable, Laura knew that. The pimply youth was stronger than her, no doubt faster than her and there was not even the remotest possibility of being able to affect an escape. Aside from which, even if she had managed to elude her lustful kidnapper, she would still have been imprisoned on his brother's farmland, in the middle of nowhere.

So she whispered a hesitant, resentful 'yes' in reply to his question, and hoped her captor wouldn't be too zealous in his assault on her butthole.

As Peter hovered behind her, his cock twitching near the entrance to her rectum, Laura tried to rationalise her anxiety. She had, after all, been used in her back passage before; so now she was going to be used there again. So what? She'd simply thrust her bottom backwards and forwards as feverishly as possible in an effort to make her lust-crazed mount spend more quickly. She lowered her head and pushed her caned buttocks higher into the air, hoping the readjustment would make her anus peel open a little more, reducing the probable discomfort when Peter pushed his penis in there.

"Ask me to do it," the bespectacled youth demanded.

Don't resist, she thought to herself, just go with the flow. "Fuck me in the ass, Peter," she murmured.

Laura heard a terrible cracking sound and felt a sharp pain high up her left buttock. "Where are your manners?" the youth demanded, and slapped her firmly again. "Now ask me once more!"

"Please fuck me in the ass, Peter."

Another fierce slap, this time to the upper portion of her right bottom-cheek. "You will address me as 'sir'," the adolescent commanded.

"Please fuck me in the ass, sir."

Two hard slaps then, delivered once again to the upper, easily accessible portions of Laura's bottom, this time across both buttocks. "Ask me to fuck you in your ass."

"Please fuck me in my ass, sir."

"Head down, keep your hands around your ankles at all times. Move, even so much as twitch, and it will be more cane."

Shit, commanded to keep still! So there would be absolutely no chance at all of quickening up the ass-fuck by her own active participation. The American felt a shiver of fear course through her. She resolved to remain perfectly still throughout the ordeal, to let him use her bottom-hole for his gratification without her making so much as a murmur in response. Avoiding another beating, that was the task on which she had to concentrate.

"Now, tell me again what I'm going to do to you," Peter demanded.

"You're going to fuck me in my ass, sir."

Laura felt the youth's cock press against her anus. A gentle push and the tip forced its way past her ring of resistant muscle. Peter clasped her hips to provide himself with greater leverage and thrust his groin forward.

Laura's eyes began to water as she felt the thick cock burrow its way into her bottom-hole.

"Keep still," he reminded her, his thighs pressing against her scorched buttocks. He was soon buried to the hilt within her anus, and no doubt ready to thrust away wildly inside the tight, slithery channel until he reached his climax, no matter how long it took. Laura bit down on her lip and reminded herself of her resolution to remain in position, to avoid angering her tormentor in any way.

Peter began to thrust then; firm, long strokes that ploughed deep into her bottom, threatening to tickle her very bowels. Laura couldn't help but grimace as the terrible defilement continued. Her anus felt as though it were certain to split open. The inner walls of her rectum were cruelly stretched by the burrowing monstrosity as it explored the secrets of her darkest orifice.

She felt the lustful bottom-fucker's thighs slam time and time again against her sore buttocks, and found herself gasping and choking as the furious, pistoning cock surged into her bumhole. She clenched her sphincter muscle in a desperate attempt to milk the wicked demon as it relentlessly scoured her bowels.

The bizarre, moonlit bottom-fuck continued for what seemed to Laura an eternity. Courageously, she held her doubled-over position throughout, her face flushing red, her naked breasts jiggling uncontrollably. Not even for an instant did she relax her firm grip on her ankles, or succumb to the punishment-earning urge to push her buttocks back; to meet the oncoming anal-ravager and finish him off fast.

Peter was grunting now. He drove his cock into her anus so hard that, with every powerful stroke, she gasped and wheezed and prayed for the eye-watering torment to be brought to a swift conclusion.

Eventually, she felt the first hot jet of spend splash against the inner walls of her rectum. Then the thick cock throbbing as it continued to pump its seed within her. And finally, mercifully, she felt the grotesque monster being carefully withdrawn from her cum-flooded bottom-hole, leaving her gasping for breath and near-delirious with relief.

12

Laura lay on her bunk, caressed by occasional gentle waves of sleep, and attempted to recover her composure following the ordeal in the woods.

She had hoped that, after spending within her, Peter would have satisfied his lustful urges and allowed her to return to the dormitory. Instead, he chose to prolong the American's moonlit agony, once again picking up his discarded cane from its resting place in the thick grass. He dragged her across the glade to a wooden fence which ran along the perimeter of an enormous field.

Laura was then told to bend herself over the middle beam of the fence. The adolescent lashed her another half-dozen times with his thick length of rattan.

The thrill of again whipping her naked bottom reawakened his sexual desire. The captive American soon found her legs pushed wide apart and the youth's thick erection once more plundering her sopping wet bottom-hole.

It was fingers clutching at her hair that deprived Laura of further fitful sleep. What now, she thought to herself. It was still dark; the other women in the dormitory were continuing to slumber. Why was she being woken up?

Fear suddenly gripped her as she recalled the ordeal of her first night on the Farm. Surely it wasn't going to happen again, not that night of all nights? Not after the torment she'd suffered secretly at the hands of Peter.

"Down from your bunk," commanded a heavy-set overseer, further urging her to do his bidding with a yank of her hair and a sharp tug on her arm. From the moment Laura's feet touched the tiled floor, it was as though everything happened at double-pace. The heavy-set overseer was accompanied by a wiry colleague, who stood nearby repeatedly rapping his cane against the open palm of his left hand. "Assume the position against the bedpost," he instructed. The bigger brute gave Laura a firm push, chivvying her along with a low-growled command to 'be quick about it'.

The American clasped the top of the bedpost and shuffled her feet backwards, arching her back and thrusting out her bottom, just as she did every morning and evening. The wiry guardsman's cane struck her once across the buttocks.

Even before the pain had coursed through her, even before she'd had time to properly register the impact of the stroke, the heavy-set overseer had grabbed her by the arm and ushered her towards the door.

Out into the open air, Laura was swiftly frog-marched around the back of the dormitory building and across the open yard to the cubicles. The two stern-faced overseers swung her round and pushed her down onto one of the toilets.

"Strain!" snapped the wiry cane-wielder. "Fast!"

Then hands were clutching her arms again, hauling her from the seat and dragging her out of the cubicle and over to the rubber hoses. Laura's mind was whirling, finding it impossible to come to terms with the speed at which everything was happening.

The bigger brute grasped her by the hair and bent her over, clamping her head between his must-scented thighs. Laura squealed with surprise as a jet of cold water was pumped into her exposed bottom cleft. She began twisting and turning her hindquarters, frantically attempting to avoid the unexpected hosing down. The water lashed at her bumhole and her sex, and splashed her hot buttocks until the whole of her bottom was soaked.

As soon as she was released from her doubled-over position, the American was again firmly gripped by the two overseers, and escorted to the side of the building, where she was bundled into a small cage on the back of a horse-drawn cart. The route the rickety wagon took was a familiar one. Back along the track beside Fields One, Two and Three, and then further still, down narrow winding lanes, through a small coppice and once again out onto uneven track. Finally, the wagon driver drew the gently ambling horse to a halt outside the Farmhouse.

He stepped down, wandered to the back of the cart and unfastened the cage door.

"Get out!"

By the time the American had dropped to the dusty ground, the door of the Farmhouse had been opened. It was Esther, the kitchen maid who Laura had witnessed being mercilessly beaten by the sadistic Gerda, who stood silhouetted in the doorway.

"In!" commanded the wagon driver. Her mind grappling to understand what was happening to her, Laura made her way across the yard to the Farmhouse, where she was ushered inside by the sympathetically smiling Esther.

The sight which met her eyes was peculiar indeed. Seated on two wooden-backed chairs, side-by-side but with approximately six feet separating them, were Hans and Gerda. The grim-looking siblings were staring malevolently at Laura, and in-so-doing were casting their gaze beyond a third—and startling—figure, who occupied the space in front of and between them. The figure, unmistakable to the American in spite of having his back turned to her, was Peter.

The lank-haired adolescent was standing virtually naked in front of his older brother and sister, his head disconsolately bowed. A pair of pyjama trousers, tangled at his ankles, were his only concession to wearing clothing.

138

"So nice of you to join us," said Gerda, a slight smile playing around her tightly drawn lips. "Did you manage to get any sleep after your night-time cavorting?"

The question impacted on Laura's mind with the force of a cane-stroke on her bottom. So, the grim pair knew what had happened. They knew all about what Peter had done to her.

In truth, she reasoned as her mind struggled to collate the new information, it would've been silly to imagine otherwise, even for a moment. Quite obviously, there was absolutely nothing which happened within the grounds of the Farm that Gerda and Hans didn't find out about.

The question was, how had they found out? The guardsman at the dormitory had still been slumbering when Peter had led Laura back from the woods. The youth had drugged his coffee flask the evening before, using sleeping pills he'd found in the Farmhouse.

So the guard certainly hadn't reported them.

Maybe there had been someone watching, after all; someone enjoying the sight of a grown woman being thrashed and violated by a pimple-infested adolescent. Or maybe there'd been video cameras hidden in the trees. Or was there some sort of night patrol? Had he heard the cane strokes, or been alerted by Laura's pain-wracked gasps and whimpering?

"I asked you a question!"

Gerda's growled words tugged Laura back from her musings. The German's eyes stared at her intently from beneath angrily furrowed brows. "Did you get any sleep?"

Forget how they found out about what had happened, Laura urged herself. She needed to concentrate on what was happening in the present, to do whatever she had to do to save her ass from another lashing.

"A little," she mumbled.

Gerda turned her gaze towards Esther, who was standing near Laura's right shoulder, waiting to do her mistress's bidding. "Smack her bottom," the German instructed her serving girl.

Esther gave Laura's left buttock a little slap. "Harder than that, girl!" the mistress demanded, "Or it will be the knout for you!" Urged on by the threat of another severe thrashing, the serving maid swung her arm at Laura's bottom-cheek again, her small palm cracking firmly against the tenderised flesh.

"Speak up, bitch-dog!" the seated mistress commanded Laura.

"A little."

Again, Gerda looked towards Esther, this time conveying instruction with a gentle nod of her head. Laura winced as the serving girl's palm slapped against her left bumcheek once more.

"Call me mistress!" bellowed the imperious German. "Now answer me again: did you get any sleep?"

"A little… mistress."

"I think you had better tell us what happened with Peter during the night."

It was Hans who spoke now, coolly eyeing the American up and down as he carefully adjusted his glasses. Laura shuffled uncomfortably. She was unnerved by the way in which he was regarding her. She was used to being viewed on the Farm as little more than a piece of meat; just another bottom to be whipped.

Perhaps she was reading too much into it, but she had a suspicion that, for once—however disinterestedly—Hans was actually taking notice of her, admiring her womanly charms. Silly though it was, Laura found herself hoping the grim-faced German didn't find them wanting.

"Peter came for me," she began, "and took me into the woods."

"What did he do then?"

Laura hardly knew what to say. She couldn't even comprehend, let alone come to terms with the peculiar situation in which she found herself. What had Peter told them, she wondered. What should she tell them—surely her story wouldn't match his; the spotty shit was bound to have lied.

And even if she told them what actually had happened, would they believe her anyway?

Perhaps the most baffling mystery, though, was why Peter should be standing bare-assed in front of his older brother and sister.

What the hell was going on?

There were just too many questions unanswered, Laura reasoned to herself. The best thing she could do was tell the truth and hope that Hans and Gerda were satisfied with her account of events.

"He beat me," she said.

"With what?"

"A cane."

"And then?"

Laura felt her stomach tighten and her throat become suddenly dry. She didn't know if she could manage to describe what the greasy youth had done to her then; didn't know if her sense of shame would allow her to actually form the necessary words.

"He—he —"

As she attempted to stammer her answer, Laura saw Gerda gently nod her head in the direction of Esther. The serving girl reacted swiftly to her mistress's silent command, once again smacking Laura on her bottom.

"Come on, bitch-dog!" the tight-lipped German woman barked. "Tell us what he did to you!"

"He used me in my bum." Laura blurted the words without really thinking about them, and was both relieved and pleasantly surprised to have so succinctly summarised the dreadful experience.

"Peter says that you were trying to escape."

"That's not true!" The little bastard, Laura thought to herself. But then, in all honesty, what had she expected him to say? That he'd felt real horny, so he'd whipped her buns and stuck it up her ass?

Not a chance.

"I was asleep. Peter came in and put a collar on me. Then he took me into the wood."

"Did you perform oral sex on him?"

Shit! Laura felt her heart begin to pound like a hammer. She began to tremble gently. She knew she couldn't afford to lie—what if they had been watching, or had irrefutable video evidence? —But at the same time, she knew she'd be incriminating herself by admitting to sucking the little cretin.

Another smack on her bottom.

The slaps were getting harder. Esther was obviously warming to her new dominant role.

"Did you perform oral sex on Peter? I will not ask you again!"

"Yes, mistress."

"Why?"

"To try and stop him from beating me."

"Peter says you have been making eyes at him and acting like a slut."

"I haven't even seen him since the day I arrived here— not until last night."

Silence prevailed, Hans and Gerda gazing coldly at Laura and then at the recalcitrant adolescent. It was Hans who spoke next:

"Very well. It is quite clear to both myself and Gerda

that some form of discipline is required here, to rectify the crimes that have been committed during the night."

At the German's words, Laura's stomach began to churn. She had known, of course, that her chances of escaping punishment were slim—beatings were prescribed for even the slightest indiscretion on the Farm, as she had found to her cost—but the realisation that her disciplining was suddenly at hand induced within her a terrible anxiety, a mind-blanking feeling of terror as she awaited her sentencing.

"Therefore," the big German continued, "you are both to be spanked, right here, right now, by myself and my sister." He adjusted his glasses once again and shifted his position slightly on the wooden chair. "Come here, Peter," he said, beckoning his younger brother with his finger.

The youth shuffled across to the powerful German, his movements rather comically hindered by the presence of the pyjama trousers twisted at his ankles. Hans took hold of the adolescent's arm and steered him to the side of the chair. With a gentle tug, he encouraged Peter to lean forward, and the youth—obviously realising there was no escaping the thrashing he was to receive—sensibly lowered himself across his brother's knee.

With his palms resting on the cold stone floor of the kitchen to support himself, and his legs splayed out to the other side of Hans, Peter's round white bottom was beautifully presented for his brother's attentions.

Laura was a little bemused as to why Gerda hadn't called her over. She'd assumed that, with two available knees, and two bare bottoms to be disciplined, she would be enduring her punishment at the same time as Peter. Yet Gerda had angled herself around a little and was lounging against the back of the chair, obviously eager to watch her younger brother receiving his comeuppance.

Hans started moving his palm across the soft white flesh of Peter's buttocks, as though smoothing them down in preparation for what was to come. Then, just as Laura began to think that Hans had perhaps thought better of beating his adolescent brother, he lifted his hand from the soft surface of Peter's bottom.

Smack, smack, smack.

The palm drove against the upturned buttocks three times, stinging first the right cheek, then the left, then landing across the fleshy underside of both gently trembling hemispheres.

Peter writhed, almost imperceptibly, as if unwilling to give his brother the satisfaction of knowing that the heavy spanks had stung.

Smack, smack, smack.

More firm slaps, following the same pattern—first right, then left, then across both buttocks. The spanks cascaded against the quivering cheeks.

Laura stood motionless; her eyes fixed on the scene, and felt a sudden, rising urge to feel her own clitoris. The spotty brat who'd so cruelly beaten and sodomised her was now stretched out in ridiculous fashion across his elder brother's knee, his pyjama trousers twisted at his ankles, his buttocks bare and reddening beneath the powerful, spanking palm of the unforgiving Hans; it was a scene by which Laura couldn't help but be excited. Her groin began to ache. It was all she could do to resist the temptation to let her hand wander between her legs, to start playing with herself.

She knew she was wet there; she could almost feel the flood tides gathering, desperate to burst her banks. Christ alone knew what would happen to her ass if she was caught diddling herself, though!

She watched the big German's hand flashing through the air, dropping onto Peter's buttock flesh, slapping it, burning it.

Smack, smack, smack.

The youth's buttocks wobbled and shook.

Oh, how Laura needed to touch her clit! To play with herself! But she knew if she did, she would climax instantly, would probably crumple to the cold stone floor, and incur the wrath of the terrible two. Peter's bottom was a burning red. The flesh looked raw and flashed like a beacon as his body twisted and turned, attempting to fight free of Hans's cruel ministrations.

The sound of Gerda snapping her fingers diverted Laura's lust-filled attentions from the spanking scene. The dour-looking German woman had shifted around on her seat again and was beckoning towards her with a long and bony finger. The American felt a terrible anxiety clutch hold of her. Her head was spinning; unable to properly process the physical sensations she was feeling. Sick with trepidation, she nevertheless couldn't ignore the exquisite stabs of excitement that fired her loins, making her burn with a lustfulness she had never before known.

Urged on by another stinging slap from the attendant Esther, Laura moved across the kitchen floor to her fate. Gerda had tugged up her leather skirt in readiness for her victim's arrival across her alabaster-white thighs.

Much to her chagrin, Laura felt another thrill course through her as she glimpsed the German woman's bulging, hairless mons; pouting, pink and untroubled by the attentions of any undergarment.

Although no longer able to look, she could hear, and see from the corner of her eye, the spanking that was proceeding on the chair next to Gerda's. She draped her sun-kissed body across the German's white flesh, feeling foolish as she lowered herself, then—shamefully she knew—excited, as her abdomen pressed against her

145

punisher's shapely thighs.

Then she felt ridiculous, as the full shame of her posture became apparent. Her bare bottom was thrusting up towards Gerda's face, her hands and feet resting against the floor. It was hard not to feel as though she were eight years old.

And it was this feeling, Laura knew, that made the situation seem so different; that set it apart from the impromptu beatings she'd endured from the strong right arms of a dozen or more brutish overseers. The cane had lashed her countless times, cutting into her bottom for the gratification of men who were violent, sadistic; who treated her as though she were no better than an animal.

Now, sprawled across Gerda's knees, the sound of Hans's palm slapping against Peter's bottom ringing in her ears, Laura felt somehow as though there were a delicious, almost sexual, excitement attached to the punishment. It was as if she and Peter were indeed small eight-year-old children, bent over the knees of their parents to be punished for some childish misdemeanour or other. And half-concealed somewhere deep within that strange, inexplicable imagining, was a new feeling for Laura; a comforting feeling that perhaps she were being punished by someone who actually cared about her, who was going to beat her because she deserved it.

An image floated into her mind, of Esther the kitchen maid—stretched along the bench, legs fastened wide apart to better allow Gerda to lash her buttocks and sex— and for a moment, Laura could have wept. It was silly to think, even for a second, that the cunning, vindictive Gerda could actually care about her. If anything, she was more cruel than the crude and bludgeoning overseers. She enjoyed humiliating Laura, enjoyed the mind games she played with the American; thrilled to Laura's impotence.

And Laura wasn't a young child, appealing though it was in a sense to pretend; she was twenty-eight. She hated lying across Gerda's knee; she was convinced of that—even though the juices gathered along her hot love-slit told a different story.

But she was sure she hated it.

How couldn't she? How couldn't any respectable twenty-something woman hate being bare-bottomed over another woman's knee, about to be spanked? No, the canings had been painful, her bottom had burned with soreness, but at least she'd been bent over and beaten with an implement; at least she'd been able to feel that, in some way, she was nothing more than another ass, to be beaten because she was there to beat.

But Gerda, the bitch; Gerda was different altogether. She wanted to humiliate her, to hurt her in her mind as well as across her buttocks; to reduce her to a snivelling, grovelling submissive.

The German began to slap her bottom then, her palm folding perfectly around Laura's pert, beautifully shaped cheeks.

The American started to wriggle soon after the spanking began. She kicked her legs and squirmed around, desperately trying to avoid the descending hand, but Gerda held her firmly in place.

The marks of her recent beatings gradually disappeared beneath the new layer of redness which suffused the full expanse of Laura's quivering cheeks. She yelped and squealed, and begged Gerda to stop, promising to be good.

"You've been a naughty girl and I'm going to spank you soundly," the German retorted as she warmed to her task, her palm continuing to dispense stinging spanks as she spoke. "You must learn, bitch-dog, that if you are going to be naughty, then your buttocks will be bared, you'll be put across my knee and your bottom will be spanked until you've been taught a lesson."

"Ow! Please! Stop—stop it! I won't do it again! Just—Ow! —don't smack me any more! Please, Mistress—please! Slap my legs if you have to, but don't spank my bum any more!"

Even as she kicked and bucked wildly, and Gerda's hand descended time after time against her bottom, Laura thought how silly she sounded, pleading like a schoolgirl for her punishment to end. She wanted to be that little girl, God how she wanted to! She hoped the gruesome Gerda beating her not because the German was a heartless dominatrix, but because she actually cared about Laura.

She wailed and threshed around like a baby, and as she was spanked, she felt a terrible, crushing yearning, a desire to be accepted into Gerda's charge there in the farmhouse where she reigned supreme, to know that she would never again be thrashed by sweat-stained brutes and made to take their filthy dicks in her ass. If there was truly no escape from the Farm, then please God let her stay in the farmhouse, where perhaps she could become a cherished addition to the staff, and where the spankings she endured would be firm yet fair.

She was almost delirious with emotion, that much was obvious!

As Laura jiggled around on Gerda's knee, she was aware of her secrets flashing into view. Her feet kicked outwards and she could feel her love slot, drenched in the silvery juices of desire, folding open. Gerda's fingers lapped at the soft lips of the American's sex, stinging the skin surrounding her ripe pink slit with firm and perfectly delivered slaps.

The American began to kick her feet against the floor and scream, abandoning herself entirely to the dreadful shame of getting her bare bottom spanked.

"I hope that will teach you!" snapped the German woman at length, clutching Laura's buttocks and squeezing them cruelly before roughly wrenching them apart. "Be a bad girl again and I will have Hans fuck this little asshole of yours until he splits it wide open!"

She sent Laura tumbling from her knee, the American's elbows cracking against the stone floor as she landed. The impact finally jolted from her the ridiculous notion that Gerda was anything other than a calculating, merciless sadist.

Breasts pressed against the stonework, her body trembling, buttocks wracked with pain, Laura could hear the sniffling sound of Peter sobbing behind her. She looked over her shoulder to where the youth lay in his twisted pyjama trousers, his bottom a burning red.

"To bed with you, Peter!" snapped Hans, "After breakfast, you will be put to work in the fields, in your shirt and your little shorts, and you will spend the day finding what it is like to be a field worker. Be smart. Be fast to 'present' when you are told. I will ask the overseers how you perform. Make me proud of you, or I will have to beat you with my cane this evening."

"And you!" Gerda barked, gently digging her shoe into Laura's rib. "Your time in the Field is at an end. The Sinfinder rides out for you today, to claim you for his circus of slaves. You have learned how to take beatings, how to obey; next, you will be taught how to perform, how to delight an expectant audience.

"Outside, the wagon awaits you. Hans will take you to the place where you are to be handed over to the Sinfinder.... And God help your very soul if you fail him."

13

It wasn't the Sinfinder who came for Laura, but two of his men. Big brutish thugs with the stench of sweat about them. They unfastened her naked body from the tree trunk where Hans had left her, and bundled her into a smaller, rickety wagon than the one in which she had arrived. The journey which followed seemed inordinately long, an ordeal drawn out even further for Laura by the terrible, gnawing sense of dread that ate away at her.

The house was foreboding; a huge, tumbledown relic from a bygone century, ill-kept and darkly grim. The enormous oak door creaked open at her arrival, and a naked, big-breasted woman beckoned Laura and her two lumbering escorts inside.

The woman led them along the hallway and down a winding flight of stairs. There was a noticeable drop in temperature the further they descended, and Laura couldn't help but feel her sense of foreboding was in no sense misplaced.

When they reached the bottom, the woman gently edged open a large, oak-panelled door. She touched the American on the elbow, encouraging her into the room. Laura's senses drank in the scene which met her. The dingy cellar was populated with people, all seated in a semi-circle, their eyes turned towards her.

There were a number of men present, but the group mainly consisted of women. Opposite the door, a high-backed chair rested against the wall. The woman who sat there, like the woman who had led Laura into the cellar, was completely naked. She was in her late thirties, Laura estimated, her stern, sharp-featured face framed by a shock of dark red, shoulder-length hair. She looked imperious and sat with her legs crossed, looking Laura up and down. "Welcome. My name is Kathy," she said.

Laura cleared her throat, and offered a tentative 'hello'.

If this new woman were anything at all like Gerda, the American knew she would do well to be polite. "When you address me, you will call me Mistress," the woman continued, the faintest of smiles crossing her lips. "The Sinfinder has asked me to make you feel at home. He wishes to apologise to you for not being present himself, but you will meet him soon enough, I think. Now…" she paused, carefully sizing Laura up "…without further delay, I think you should be introduced to your new regime. Forget all about the Farm now, bitch-dog, with its crude, indiscriminate discipline," she said sternly. "Here, you will truly learn how to obey. How to please."

Her gaze wandered towards first one, then a second of the assembled throng.

"Now, I believe, Stephanie and Katie, it's your turn to provide the entertainment. This is one of the rooms in which we train subjects how to please, Laura," she said, gazing at the American. Laura stood flanked by the muscular beasts who'd brought her to the dark and dingy house. "It is here that we first receive new recruits; where we first initiate them into their new life as one of the Sinfinder's circus bitches. And when it comes to initiation," she paused again, and ran her fingers through her thick red hair, "we really do believe there is no time like the present."

The Mistress turned towards one of the seated women to whom she had earlier spoken. "Well now, Stephanie, do you think you can possibly incorporate our new-found friend into your little performance."

"I think so, yes. It shouldn't be too much of a problem."

The woman who'd replied to the Mistress's question sat just a couple of yards away from Laura. Legs crossed, hands clasped together resting against her lap, Stephanie was most notable for the blondness of her long, wavy hair and for the huge size of her breasts, immense and disproportionate with the rest of her trim, well-shaped physique.

"And what exactly do you have for us tonight?"

"I'm playing a headmistress and Katie is a trouble-making teenage tearaway." The Mistress ran her fingers through her hair once more and readjusted her position. The vaguest of smiles flashed across her face. "Well, given my position as the Sinfinder's right-hand lady," she said, "I shall watch your performance with interest, Stephanie."

Ripples of appreciative, sycophantic laughter emanated from the semi-circle. The Mistress's gaze flitted towards a young woman seated opposite Stephanie. "Katie," she said at length, "I think perhaps you should play the parent of a terribly wilful child, who, of course, can then be played by Laura."

"Yes Mistress," Katie replied. Laura could feel her heart beating like a drum. Her breaths were coming in short, sharp gasps. Suddenly, she knew what her fate was to be, knew that she too was going to be once again disciplined; and knew that, in looking at Stephanie, she was looking at the executor of her punishment.

"Prepare Laura, gentlemen."

The instruction caused a further notable increase in the speed at which Laura's heart was pounding. She was delivered into the sole custody of the brute standing at her right shoulder, his arms encircling her, pinning hers into place at her side. The other sweat-caked beast moved purposefully across the room to a large dust-laden chest made from oak wood. He opened the heavy lid, delved inside and pulled out a number of objects which, in the gloom, Laura was unable to identify.

He returned to her side and deposited the items on the stone floor. The man who was holding her adjusted his grip, enabling him to liberate one of his arms from the task of immobilising Laura. His freed hand pressed against her forehead, guiding her head back until she was staring at the stark, glowering light bulb that hung from a frazzled cord about two feet below the ceiling.

The man in front of her lifted something from the floor and she felt his hand clasp her jaw. Fingers pressed at the flesh of her jowls, teasing her mouth open. Laura felt a small rubber ball pressed against her lips and nudged in between her teeth. The ball was attached to a strip of leather, the ends of which were then pulled tight around either side of her head and secured at the base of her skull.

She bit into the rubber and tried to move her tongue, hoping to get sufficient leverage to push the ball from her mouth. Her efforts were futile; she was comprehensively gagged. The man in front of her was at her feet then, snapping iron manacles around each of her ankles. The manacles were linked together by a short chain and ensured that any steps she were to take would be inhibited and uncomfortable. Handcuffs were snapped about her wrists; a padded leather collar, from which hung a short length of cord, was fitted loosely around her neck.

The Mistress clapped her hands together once, and Stephanie and Katie stood up. Stephanie walked across to a chair that rested in the centre of the semi-circle and sat down. Katie moved across to Laura. The two thugs who had been restraining the American shifted away, allowing the young woman to take hold of her. Katie clasped the cord hanging from the neck collar and gently tugged, guiding the bound woman towards the centre of the room.

Laura winced as she shuffled forward, the manacles chaffing her skin as she tentatively placed one leg in front of the other. By the time she reached the seated Stephanie, she was aware that she had emerged into the full glare of the naked light bulb, and fancied she could almost feel its warmth kissing the skin of her exposed bottom.

Stephanie looked stern. Her long blond hair cascaded about her shoulders and chest, partly concealing the bulging cleavage that separated her massive breasts. She sat with her legs crossed, her long skirt having tumbled open where its material was daringly split to the top of her thigh. The fingers of one hand toyed with the variety of glittering rings that adorned the other.

"Now, Mrs Steele," she said, suddenly adopting the persona of a scowling Headmistress, "I have asked you to come to my study this evening so that we can discuss your errant daughter Laura. Once again, she has been bullying the other girls in her class and stealing money from them. Furthermore, when the deputy head did her rounds of the dormitories last night, Laura was found in bed with another girl, sucking on her breasts and fondling her cunt."

Laura shuffled beside Katie. She felt sick to the very pit of her stomach.

"I'm sorry, Miss Belt." Katie's voice was almost tearful. She stood beside Laura, her head bowed in shame, her dark hair tumbling about purposefully-hunched shoulders. "Laura is such a difficult child, and being a single parent, it isn't easy to keep her under control."

"I am not interested in your excuses, Mrs Steele," Stephanie snapped, her face hardening as she glared at the recalcitrant Katie, "I am interested only in ensuring that there is no repeat of these incidents. You have clearly failed in your duty to Laura and, therefore, I am holding you as responsible for her shameful behaviour as she herself is. It pains me greatly to have to say this, but I am afraid that there seems little alternative but to discipline you as well as her."

Katie looked up suddenly, her eyes wide and imploring as they met those of the seated woman. "Oh Miss Belt, please—no! Please don't punish me as well as my daughter! I'm sorry for being such a bad mother, really I am! I'm begging you not to discipline me too!"

"I'm sorry, but you leave me no choice." Stephanie uncrossed her legs and straightened out the thin material of her long, flowery skirt. "Get across my knee this instant, Mrs Steele!"

"Oh please, Miss Belt! Please don't! If you have to punish me, can't you give me a cut of the cane across my hand, or make me write out a thousand lines?"

"Don't be ridiculous!" Stephanie growled, clasping Katie's wrist and encouraging the younger woman to her side. "Punishment is decreed on the bare bottom. It is the only way any woman will learn how to behave and it is the only form of discipline in which I believe. Now do not make me any angrier than I am. Place your body over my knee right away!"

Katie draped herself across the waiting legs. Stephanie placed a hand on the back of her victim's head and guided it downwards, so that the young woman's nose was virtually touching the stone floor. Adjusting the weight of her captive slightly, she tugged at the short leather skirt the upturned woman was wearing, hitching it up to her waist to reveal a pair of semi-exposed buttocks.

Without a second's delay, Stephanie snatched Katie's tiny briefs down to her knees, laying bare the expanse of superbly rounded bottom flesh that she was about to punish. "Right, Mrs Steele," she said purposefully, "let's see if we can't teach you a lesson about good parenting that you'll never forget. Perhaps if you had been more diligent in placing Laura over your own knee, you wouldn't now find yourself in this ridiculously humiliating situation."

In one confident movement, Stephanie raised her arm above her head and brought her hand flashing down, slapping against Katie's exposed right buttock. The woman squealed and wriggled in response; her bum flesh, quivering from the slap, jiggled all the more because of her own frantic contortions.

"It is shameful that a grown woman need be placed across my knee. I shall have to call you back into my office at a later date in order to administer a caning to your shameful moons!"

Stephanie's hand spanked the wobbling cheeks in front of her. The smacks descended with such regularity that the flesh of Katie's bottom was still trembling from the previous spank when the next one arrived. She twisted and turned across the blonde woman's legs, her feet threshing the air and her buttocks burning an ever-deeper crimson.

"Oh Miss Belt, please!" she squealed, "please don't spank me any more! I'll be good, I promise! My bottom's so sore! Oh please, Miss, I beg you to stop beating me!"

"You are a shameless little hussy!" spat Stephanie from between clenched teeth. Her hand continued to slap against the hot flesh of Katie's round bottom. "I will beat your errant bum-end until you have learned your lesson. I have a strong right arm, my girl, so don't think your naughty big bottom is going to escape its just desserts!"

Katie continued to squeal throughout the remainder of her punishment. Her buttocks quivered like jellies as she writhed and twisted across Stephanie's thighs. When she was finally allowed to stand up, she staggered momentarily before steadying herself. Her hands clasped her spanked buttocks as her chest heaved in and out. She was inhaling and exhaling huge gulps of air in a desperate attempt to calm herself down, to satisfy her lungs' greedy desire for oxygen. Her exertions had tired her and she seemed dazed for several minutes. Her hair was plastered to her face by the saliva that had dribbled from her mouth as she'd thrashed around wildly; a rabid animal, seeking salvation from the stinging spanks. Her cheeks were flushed and wet, her eyes tear-stained.

Stephanie's face remained as cold and impassive as ever. "And now for you, Laura." It seemed as though everybody in the room was holding their breath. Laura was certain they must all have witnessed Katie being spanked before at some point—it seemed likely that everybody, except—perhaps—the Mistress, took their turn in having their bare buttocks punished—so the scene which had just been played out, while titillating and erotic, didn't have the element of novelty which the prospect of Laura's own punishment provided for the assembled throng.

Stephanie flicked back her skirt, revealing her shapely legs—sheathed in a pair of inexpensive tights—and her crotch, pouting from within her panties. "If you're going to wriggle as much as your mother," she said, continuing with the role-play, "I am not going to risk damaging this rather lovely skirt. Now come here, you little tart!"

Stephanie leaned forward and took the neck collar cord in her hand, roughly dragging Laura towards her. The chain between the captive woman's ankle irons dragged across the stone surface of the floor as she staggered towards her destiny. "Your daughter has been bound and gagged since last night's incident, Mrs Steele," Stephanie said. "Bound ankles make it more difficult for her to move unnoticed and unheard to other girls' beds. Manacled wrists inhibit her ability to satisfactorily fondle her classmates' cunts, while a gag in her mouth stops her from sucking and licking at the naked titties of innocent young girls. These should also prove efficacious for this particular situation, ensuring your wanton daughter can be thoroughly and comprehensively punished for her crimes with the minimum of fuss."

Stephanie's bejewelled hand clutched at Laura's arm and she felt herself being steered over the waiting knee, lowered slowly and gently to allow her the opportunity to position her handcuffed hands in such a way as to support herself. Her palms rested against the floor to one side of 'Miss Belt', her toes and the balls of her feet settled against the ground to the other.

The flat of Stephanie's hand against the back of her head forced Laura to lower her upper body further down towards the floor, so that the side of her face pressed against the cold stone slabs. In this position, her bare buttocks rose high in the air, just as she knew 'Miss Belt' wanted them.

"Now let's have a look at what we've got here," Miss Belt said, and Laura felt a hand take hold of each of her buttocks. Her doubled-up position had already opened up the cleft between her cheeks; Miss Belt's hands exposed the valley entirely, plying Laura's buttocks wide apart until the flesh was fully stretched. Laura felt a draft of cold air kiss the soft, slightly revealed inner flesh of her anus, and knew that Miss Belt was closely inspecting her wrinkled orifice. Her buttocks were slapped together again, and Laura felt momentary relief, the humiliation of having her bottom-mouth exposed beneath the stark glare of the light bulb slowly subsiding.

"You are a shameful child, Laura," murmured Miss Belt threateningly, "and you are going to get your bottom thoroughly spanked." Laura felt the slightest of movements beneath her as Miss Belt adjusted the position of her legs. The smooth nylon of her tights caressed the fronts of the bound woman's thighs and stomach. And then she heard a crack, reverberating sharply around the stone cellar. She was aware of a hand momentarily resting against her right buttock, and then she felt a raw, stinging pain stabbing at her bottom flesh—her second over-the-knee spanking of the morning was underway.

She murmured, and the sound slipped out from behind the rubber ball-gag wedged in her mouth. She was aware that she had wriggled her bottom in response to the slap, and hated herself for doing so. She knew that her writhing would heighten the eroticism of the role-play, increase her shame and humiliation. But she couldn't help it. The spank had taken her by surprise and made her flesh smart.

Just as had been the case earlier in the farmhouse, she really did feel like a disobedient little schoolgirl turned over the Headmistress's knee for a bare-bottom punishment. She closed her eyes tightly, until the skin of her face wrinkled and creased, and tried hard to swallow, an action inhibited by the presence of the ball-gag.

She wanted to blot out what was happening, couldn't stand the sight of the assembled observers, leaning forward on their chairs, eyes focused on her naked bottom, watching another woman spank its redness a dreadful shade of crimson. She squealed and gurgled as a second, third and fourth spank cracked against her flesh. She knew she was blushing red as her buttocks trembled like fat jellies, and whimpered as the sharp stings burned her skin.

Miss Belt held her firmly and was throwing her full weight behind every powerful slap. "This spanking will hopefully teach you that bullying and theft do not pay!" she scolded, gasping with the exertion of tanning the soft and succulent bottom that gyrated beneath her nose. "Wriggle all you like, you little whore, I've got plenty of strength left to thrash these shameful arse cheeks of yours! I'll teach you a lesson, my girl! These moons are going to be burning hot for days to come once I've finished with you!"

The dreadful scolding seemed to exacerbate Laura's sense of humiliation. It made her twist and writhe all the more feverishly as she attempted to slide off Miss Belt's voluptuous thighs and escape the slapping palm that chastised her tender bottom. "Such naughtiness is unheard of at my school!" gasped Miss Belt breathlessly, "I will spank the disobedience out of you —" smack smack, "—and turn this lovely, bare-faced bott of yours five shades of purple!"

Smack, smack, smack, smack. Laura was bucking by now, her movements wild, frenzied and outrageously sexual. The spanks continued to descend. Her bottom felt huge and swollen, stinging sore yet strangely numb. She was aware of nothing now except the smouldering flesh of her buttocks and the palm of Miss Belt's hand.

"Mrs Steele, take hold of your daughter's legs and hold her still!"—smack smack smack—"She's as wild as a mule! Hold her while I spank her bumcheeks raw!"—smack smack smack—Katie—Mrs Steele—clutched Laura's calves, clamping them into position so that the bound woman's thighs pressed against the side of Miss Belt's leg.

Smack, smack.

"That's better," sighed the make-believe Headmistress, partially relieved of the need to grapple with the writhing woman stretched out across her thighs, "Now I can concentrate all my energies on spanking Laura's botty!"

Smack, smack, smack.

Eventually, with a long, languid exhalation of breath,

Miss Belt delivered a final stinging spank to the trembling peaks of Laura's swollen mounds, her hand resting for a time afterwards across the clammy divide that separated the burning bum-hills. Laura's whole body trembled, and as she choked and gurgled on the ball-gag, tears poured along the still-wrinkled contours of her face, dripping from her chin onto the stone floor.

There was silence, save for the whimpering noises that Laura herself was making. Her bottom, sensitised to the brink of numbness by the spanking, throbbed with the sting of her chastisement. A cool kiss to her right buttock soothed the raging fever of pain a little, and she was grateful when another kiss was planted against her left cheek. The hands which had clasped her calves glided up her legs and stroked her sore bottom, gently massaging the burning skin. Again there was the feeling of soft lips, planting a wetter kiss, on the crease of flesh where her left buttock met her thigh, the region that burned most. And then another kiss, higher up the same palpitating globe. Then another, planted this time on her right buttock.

She murmured a little when she felt a moist tongue tenderly lick at her. The tongue touched the underside of her throbbing moon, caressing the sore skin, and traced a path into her semi-exposed bum-valley. The hands resting on her bottom peeled her tender cheeks apart, and the tongue tickled her anus.

Laura wriggled a little, knowing that she didn't want what was happening to her, didn't want the touch of a tongue there, in her most private, most shameful, place. But she throbbed and she ached, and her bottom burned. And Stephanie—for it was obvious by the way her punisher's hand was gently stroking her lower back, that the alter ego of Miss Belt had disappeared—would undoubtedly hold her across her legs until Katie's lips, fingers and tongue had finished their playful dalliance with her bottom.

So Laura squirmed a little and squeezed her eyes more tightly shut. And as she did so, Katie's tongue lapped at her bottom-opening, teasing the sensitive folds of clammy flesh that had gently opened like a flower bud. Lips were pressed against Laura's little 'o', a succulent kiss planted, and then the tongue returned, sliding down until it lapped against the soft pinkness of her fleshy sex.

Now she moaned; moaned and writhed in spite of herself. And as the young woman's tongue slid the length of her love slot, Laura realised that, just as she had been at the farmhouse, she was sopping wet. She could even hear the sound of her lover licking her glistening cunt and then, without warning, she was consumed, incredibly, by a shattering orgasm, ripping through her body and teasing her every nerve-ending, sending shivers up and down her spine, causing her to mash her pelvis against the silky thighs of her blonde captor.

One lash of a tongue, one touch, and Laura had been lost, her senses reeling, her mind and body enraptured. Her buttocks tightened, muscles twitching, and her pelvis began to buck as the orgasm gradually subsided. She slithered, wasted and broken, from her punishment position, buttocks contorting as she sank to the floor. And all around her, the only noise she could hear was the unmistakable sound of enthusiastic applause.

14

The Mistress Kathy stood up and held out her arms. Stephanie and Katie embraced her as the applause continued to echo around the dingy cellar. "Well done, girls," she commended, her hands sliding down to their bottoms and gently squeezing their flesh.

"The Sinfinder will be most pleased when I report to him. It was a delightful display, beautifully presented and excellently scripted. A real crowd pleaser. You did a wonderfully expert job on that lovely backside of..." The Mistress quizzically raised an eyebrow at the new arrival. "Laura," came the gasping response. "...that lovely backside of Laura's, Stephanie—and you certainly seemed to touch all the right buttons, Katie."

The Mistress looked beyond the two women to the semi-circle of enraptured watchers.

"Ladies and gentlemen, it's time for you to take your leave of me. The bedrooms are ready, you'll find everything you require, I'm sure. And remember, the Sinfinder will be watching; so make sure you give him a good show. Katie, would you be so kind as to explain to Laura exactly what is expected now."

"Of course, Mistress."

Katie approached the still-heaving figure of Laura, while at the same time the observers stood and formed an orderly queue in front of the Mistress. Crouching down in front of her, the brunette gently brushed a still-rolling tear from Laura's cheek. "What you need to do now," she said in a calm, soothing voice, "is to be a big girl and just follow what the rest of us do." Katie unfastened the gag and removed the ball from within Laura's mouth. "We must all say farewell to the Mistress for the time being, in the way which the Sinfinder always demands."

Laura peered through her tears towards the Mistress. The naked woman was turned away from her, moving towards her high-backed chair. Clasping its arms, the Mistress kneeled on the edge of the padded seat with her legs apart. Laura could see tufts of her thick minge hanging low from her groin. The pink swelling of her sex peeked teasingly from between the splendid, fleshy buttocks that bloomed proudly outwards, thrusting provocatively towards her assembled subjects. Laura was intrigued to see that the cheeks were criss-crossed with blotchy marks, as though the Mistress had been beaten with a thick strap.

"We must say farewell to the Mistress," Katie continued, "by each placing a kiss on her arse. This is what the Sinfinder always demands." Stephanie stood at the front of the line. When the Mistress clicked her fingers, Laura's chastiser walked purposefully forward, sank to her knees and rested her hands against the naked woman's buttocks. Gently, she peeled the savagely flogged cheeks away from each other until the deep bottom cleft was exposed to the glowering attentions of the unforgiving light bulb.

"The kiss must be full blooded, yet soft and succulent," Katie whispered, watching as Stephanie carefully pressed her face into the Mistress's bum-valley. "The kiss should be vaguely audible, and should leave the thinnest film of moisture on the Mistress's arsehole."

Stephanie planted a kiss and gently returned the buttocks to their resting place. She stood up and left the room. Katie moved forward as soon as Stephanie had closed the Mistress's bottom cleft. She peeled the buttocks gently open and tentatively pressed her puckered lips onto the rubbery surface of the woman's wrinkled 'o'.

A succulent kiss, then she too departed. Each person

in turn paid homage to the slowly moistening anus and then left the room, the taste of the Mistress's bottom-mouth heavy on their lips. Eventually, there was only the Mistress, Laura and Katie left in the room. The brunette gently nudged Laura, encouraging her to stand up and kiss the naked woman's bottom. "Go and do it now, Laura, before you make her, and more importantly, the Sinfinder, angry."

Laura wiped the dried saltwater, caused by her tears, from her face and hauled her aching body to its feet. The torture of the Farm, the new bondage torment at the hands of the Sinfinder's cohorts, had left her tired and broken, but not shattered—not yet at least; and there were some things she just could not—no, would not—do.

"No," she said calmly. "No, I'm not doing that."

"Go now," Katie urged, a tremor of anxiety evident in her voice. "Her bottom's sheathed in moisture by now; you'll hardly notice what you're doing."

"No. Not that."

"Is there a problem?" The Mistress sounded stern, impatient. She looked over her shoulder. "Where are you, Laura? Pay your respects, if you please."

"No, I won't do that."

"Your kiss then please, Katie."

Katie moved hurriedly forward, carefully lowering herself down onto her knees, and took hold of the Mistress's big buttocks. Peeling them apart, she leaned forward and pressed her mouth against the wet anus, softly erupting a delicious kiss against the puckered, volcanic aperture. She stood up and, without setting eyes on Laura again, swiftly departed the room.

The Mistress herself stood up and turned to face Laura. "By the time the Sinfinder has finished with you," she whispered, her face a mask of smouldering anger, "you

165

will know no greater pleasure than to do that which you have just refused." She dragged her long, tapering fingers through her hair and moved towards the newcomer. "Forget all thoughts of a life beyond the confines of the Sinfinder's control," she warned, taking hold of the leash and drawing Laura so close to her that their breasts touched. "You are now a possession of his circus of performing slaves." The Mistress's fingers crawled around Laura's waist, coming to rest against the flesh of her scorched bottom, "What a lovely plaything you are," she purred, "a real wildcat. I can tell by the look in your eyes."

Laura grimaced as the Mistress pinched her cheeks, twisting and rolling the spanked flesh. The American swallowed hard then, as the pinching was replaced by a series of gentle slaps, re-warming her tingling skin.

"The Sinfinder will break you, you little whore," the naked woman growled. "You have no idea what he can do to you; no idea what it is to be really punished, to be totally possessed by somebody."

A sharp slap to Laura's thigh caused her to expel a pathetic whimper. She clenched her teeth, determined it would be the last sound of suffering the woman would draw out of her.

"I'm sure you'll be interested to see what's happening in the upstairs areas of the house," the Mistress said. "You will see then what lies in store for you; the way in which you will be trained like a dog, rehearsed like a performing monkey, and then—eventually—sent out into the circus ring, into the Big Top, to perform for the Sinfinder and his audiences." She grabbed Laura by the leash and tugged. The American stumbled in the Mistress's wake, following the naked woman out of the cellar and up the stairs.

Shameful though she knew it to be, Laura was

transfixed by the magnificence of the bare buttocks in front of her. The red flesh of the beautifully rounded cheeks rolled and trembled as the Mistress climbed the staircase. They made their way along the hallway, Laura shuffling in her irons, her bottom still ablaze from the spanking she had received, her wrists sore from the constant rubbing of the handcuffs. Another flight of stairs.

Two paces along a dark dank corridor and the Mistress flung open a door. Laura peered in. A woman lay naked on a bed, her rolls of middle aged fat trembling in rhythm with the long moans that emanated from her mouth at regular intervals. Katie was naked too, her charming young bottom a ruddy red and thrust towards the ceiling, her face buried between the older woman's legs.

The Mistress closed the door. A tug of the leash and Laura shuffled after her, biting her lip as she stubbed her toe against an uneven floorboard. The naked woman opened another door. Laura's eyes were wide with fascination. Inside the room, one of the men who had been seated in the semi-circle in the cellar stood dressed in a baggy, dishevelled Victorian policeman's uniform. At the sound of the unexpected intrusion, he turned momentarily, revealing beneath his oversized helmet a flushed red face, trickling with perspiration. In his hand, he held an implement that Laura could not properly identify. Shaped like a hairbrush, but without any bristles, the item seemed to be made of thick, pliable leather. Standing in front of him, screwed into the floor, was a full-sized replica of a Victorian street lamp, exact in every detail, although much of the pole was obscured from Laura's view by the presence of the man's bulky physique.

As he shifted slightly, Laura was able to get a clear view of the lamp, and saw that there was a woman

167

fastened to it. Her arms were raised above her head and she was bound at the wrists. The white blouse she wore was torn in several places, allowing her shoulder and ribcage to peak through. She wore no skirt; her outermost layer of lower body clothing being a pair of savagely shredded tights, only the waistband of which remained fully intact.

The nylon covering her buttocks had been torn away, revealing deliciously dimpled flesh; beautifully rotund, submissively exposed, cruelly reddened. The panties she wore were so skimpy that they covered no portion of her bottom cheeks whatsoever, being little more than a narrow piece of fabric running the length of her bum cleft, the breadth of her waist and no doubt constituting little more than a tiny, triangular patch of material at her crotch.

Her hair was long and blonde. The slight angle at which the replica street lamp stood to the door meant Laura could just about see the woman's left breast; huge, magnificent and completely bare. She quickly realised that the dishevelled, tatty woman at whom she was staring was none other than Stephanie, who only minutes earlier had been administering to Laura her second bare bottom spanking of the day.

"Don't let us stop you, constable," the Mistress Kathy said to the implement-wielding man, joining in with the role-play implied by the scene, "we'll just come in and watch you mete out justice to this wanton woman, if it's all the same with you. Perhaps you could fill us in on the details."

The visitors entered the room. The Mistress directed Laura to a bed that nestled against the window, and then lounged back in a battered old armchair.

"Of course, ma'am," the police officer said. "This is a local whore who I've caught soliciting under this street lamp before. Having moved her along on a previous occasion, warning her that I wouldn't be so lenient the next time, I again found her plying her shameful trade this very evening. I am now in the process of teaching her a damn good lesson in the hope that it will assist her to mend her ways."

"Please carry on, constable," said the Mistress. "I'm sure we wouldn't wish to stand in the way of Justice."

"Thank you, ma'am. Very thoughtful of you, I'm sure."

The policeman turned his attention to the blotchy crimson bottom in front of him. Laura sat transfixed as he swung the heavy leather paddle through a vast arc, bringing it down with a fearsome splat. His victim was trying to wrench her hands free of the cord that bound them in place. Another heavy smack cracked against the jiggling bum mounds, the sound of the paddle as it scorched soft buttock flesh ringing around the room.

"You are a shameful whore," the policemen snapped, spanking the trembling cheeks again, "a shameful wicked tart!" Again he paddled the prostitute's bottom, bringing the leather down with such force that her body was mashed against the lamppost, causing her big, fleshy breasts to quiver and shake. "Let's see how many clients are interested in fucking your arse once I've paddled the flesh off it, you dirty strumpet!"

Another vigorously delivered paddle. "Bad girl!" The prostitute wailed, writhing frantically. "That's it! That's it, you filthy whore! Squeal like a piggy while I flog your wicked buns. I'll teach you a lesson you'll not forget. I'll show you!" Splat. Splat. "You'll never flash those big titties anywhere on my beat again!" Splat. Splat. "Filthy whore!" Splat. "Filthy frigging whore."

The policeman was upon her as soon as he'd delivered the final tortuous spank. One hand mauling her enormous breasts, he used the other to wrench his engorged cock from within the baggy uniform. Once done, his hand slapped against her buttocks, ripping away her panties. His fingers slipped between her legs, rubbing and fondling.

When his hand emerged it was wet with the woman's juices. He clasped his cock with the newly-glistening hand and buried it between the prostitute's thighs. She squealed and groaned as he mashed her into the lamppost again and forced her legs wide apart. A thick odour of sex mingled with the scent of sweat as the Mistress and Laura watched the policeman thrust himself in and out of the bound and flogged prostitute, his cock momentarily emerging into the outside world—sheathed in silvery juices—and then returning to the hot, sopping love trench.

The blonde woman's buttocks quivered and her breasts jiggled as though she were performing a grotesque, frenetic dance. The constable pulled himself free of the prostitute's soaking wet slot and dropped to his knees. His hands, clutching at the material of her blouse, ripped the garment free, revealing her white stomach. Fingers at her bottom, he pulled her open and spat into her cleft. He pressed his face between her cheeks and she struggled for freedom, wrapping her legs around the lamppost and desperately, futilely, attempting to climb upwards.

The policeman's hands were at her thighs, pulling her legs free of the pole, forcing them wide again. Standing up, he held the cheeks of her bottom apart and pushed his throbbing cock between them. "No!" she moaned. "No! Not there! Not like that! Please."

The sight of the policeman's body collapsing against hers was a sure sign that he had gained access to her. She howled as she was impaled, and promised to never again solicit on the copper's beat. "Too late for that, whore! I'm going to fuck your filthy arse until I split your bum cheeks right open!" the copper growled.

Hot and flushed, the prostitute pressed the side of her head against the lamppost. She was facing Laura, who could clearly see the tears rolling down the flushed cheeks, could hardly miss the grimaces of pain. But she could also detect the lust, the excitement that was etched on the blonde woman's twisted, anguished face. She could tell from her breathing that she was turned on, secretly yearning every vigorous thrust of her lover's thick muscle within her hungry bottom-mouth.

The copper began to pump her; his first savage thrust slamming her against the lamppost. Clasping her waist, he drew her lower body away from the pole, causing her head to drop, her breasts to dangle free, and extending her bound arms to the fullest extent. By forcing her into a bending position, he could impale her bottom totally, so that the complete length of his shaft was fitted inside the tight trench of her bum-pit.

"Take that, you whore-tart," he growled, thrusting right into her until his balls slapped against her well-paddled buttocks. "I'm going to shag your dirty arse and fill you up with my come. Let's see how you like a taste of this up your shit-hole!"

Laura felt the layers of perspiration building on her as she watched. The prostitute's face was screwed up and pain-ridden; her enormous breasts were bouncing in all directions, occasionally slapping against the lamppost as she was vigorously sodomised. The policeman's thick stem was pumping in and out of her tight bumhole with such fervour that uninformed onlookers could have been forgiven for thinking he was thrusting into a sopping wet, fully lubricated vagina. His muscle drove deeper and deeper, and even from across the room, Laura was aware that his breathing had changed.

"Dirty slapper!" he grunted, "Ever had a big copper's

dick up your stenching arse-pit before? Ever—" he heaved himself forward, ramming himself at the prostitute until every morsel of his cock was jammed into the clammy hole of her bottom, "—ever had a fat cock unload a big sack of come up your filthy crapper?!"

He was staggering now.

"I'm going to —" It was obvious to Laura he was close to the end. "I'm going to shag your arsehole so hard, girly, it'll split your bum in two! I'll... I'll give you something to think about, my girl, just you wait and see!"

The policeman groaned and slumped forward, crushing the prostitute into the lamppost yet again. Even though concealed by baggy trousers, it was obvious that the man's buttocks were clenching and unclenching; obvious that he was in the throes of pumping his spend deep into Stephanie's bowels.

The Mistress snapped her fingers and stood up. "Time to go," she announced, pacing like a panther to the doorway, not even bothering to check whether Laura was shuffling behind her.

Up another staircase. Kathy flung open another door. A woman was kneeling on a bed, completely naked, her curvaceous posteriors facing the door. Her legs were apart, her lush minge and glistening pink sex flesh fully exposed. Standing to each side of her were two other women. Between them, they were working her bottom over. Each wielded a rubber-soled slipper, and were slapping away at the kneeling girl's ample mounds. The bottom was quivering beautifully as it was spanked, the girl unable to suppress an almost constant flow of squeals and groans, despite the fact that she'd buried her face in a pillow.

The next room offered another startling tableau. A beautiful woman, exquisite in her slender, long-limbed glory, was naked and flat on her back on a bed. She was attended by the two brutes who had brought Laura to the house. The woman was lying across the mattress, in such a way that her head hung backwards off the bed. One of the men, kneeling on the floor behind her head, had his cock buried in her mouth. Her delectable lips were avidly sucking on the beast, seeking to draw its venom. Her legs, meanwhile, were drawn back over her head, doubling her up so that her knees hovered above her ripe little breasts. The second man was kneeling on the bed, his thick penis plunging in and out of her juicy pink sex. His fingers were tweaking her soft nipples as he thrust inside her, the open palm of his hand occasionally slapping one breast or the other, causing her to suck more furiously on the other man's penis.

The Mistress opened yet another door and ushered Laura inside. "Take a seat," she said. "Before I release you into the custody of the Sinfinder General himself, I have a few little amusements with which to regale you." Laura did as she was told, settling herself on a hard, wooden-backed chair. The Mistress clapped her hands once and then pulled up another chair next to Laura's, lowering her magnificent, well-strapped posteriors onto its padded seat and crossing her muscular white legs.

Laura looked across the gloomy room towards a door on the far side, and found herself wondering what kind of strange scene was about to unfold...

The door to the far side of the room creaked slowly open, and two shadowy figures emerged from the darkness. The figures moved slowly towards the centre of the room. Laura followed them with her eyes as her jaw sagged wide in surprise. "This is Tony," said Kathy, motioning towards the short, well-tanned male standing before them. "And this, I'm sure you'll recognise, is..."

"Sally!" Laura muttered beneath her breath.

The man named Tony smiled, and gave a sharp yank

on the cord he was holding. "Greet your friend with a cheery hello then." It was Sally to whom he spoke. The cord he held was linked to a leather collar, which in turn was snugly fastened around Sally's neck. The sudden tug forced her forward, inducing her to perform a half bow.

"Hello," she said meekly. Laura could hardly believe what she was seeing. Sally stood next to Tony encased in the most amazing garment the American had ever laid eyes on. It seemed to be made entirely of rubber, and encased her friend from neck to foot. It was too small for her, and that fact, allied to the clinging nature of the rubber, caused her physique to seem more highly toned than usual, like a taut spring ready to uncoil.

The chest area of the garment had been cut away. Sally's breasts poked through the holes, pink nipples erect as though they'd been recently stimulated. Laura could see that the rubber was biting into the flesh of her friend's bosom, making her breasts thrust out; seem bigger somehow. Sal's hair had been scraped back, gelled into place. Her face, normally so soft and attractively oval, looked pinched, as though she was struggling to breathe properly, constricted as she was by the close attentions of the rubber suit.

Tony tugged on the leash again and drew Sally towards him. He pressed his lips against hers and slipped his tongue into her mouth. Laura was surprised to see that her friend was returning her captor's attentions—though when she thought about it, what the hell else was Sal supposed to do? —and soon they were engrossed in the pleasures of a long, succulent kiss.

He pulled away from her. She tentatively edged her head forward, seeking to again lock her mouth with his. Interesting. There was no need for her to do that, Laura thought to herself. Tony's hand sounded like a pistol shot as it slapped against Sally's cheek.

"I'll decide when we kiss!" he growled, tugging on the leash and twisting her round so that she was facing away from Laura. Not for the first time since the two new people had entered the room, the American found herself gasping with surprise. The rubber suit Sally was wearing had been cut away to reveal her buttocks, jutting out temptingly and spanked a ruddy red. Laura felt her juices flowing. What was it about seeing a slapped ass that turned her on so much? Tony jerked at the leash, forcing Sally to bend forward. Her buttocks bloomed from their encasement, the cheeks folding apart slightly.

Tony's hand slapped away at the naked bottom, applying a fast beating and still continuing despite his victim's squealing and twisting. Laura watched her friend's bottom rapidly acquire a fiery crimson hue as Tony worked her over. As swiftly as it had started, the spanking stopped. Tony wrenched at the leash again, sharply swinging Sally around so that her breasts swayed backwards and forwards as she fought to retain her balance.

"I'm going to whip you now," he announced in a matter-of-fact tone.

"Please no, master," Sally pleaded. "Please don't punish my arse any more."

"Don't you like being punished on your bottom, Sally?"

An expression of fear flashed across Sally's face as she cowered before her captor; a frightened rabbit, facing menacing headlights.

"You've already made my arse hot with your hand, master," she blubbered. "I don't think I could stand more spanks." Tony laughed out loud. "I said you must be whipped, girl, not spanked like a baby. Your buttocks must be kissed by my long leather whip."

"Please master, please don't!" There was a sense of urgency in Sal's voice which Laura had never heard before. She could see that her friend's body was gently trembling inside her rubber bondage wear. She felt sure that her own cunt was getting considerably wetter as she listened to Sally grovelling to save her miserable ass.

"My bum's so sore from the spankings you've given it. I'll do anything to avoid the whip. I'm begging you not to whip my bottom, sir."

"What will you do to avoid a whipping, slave girl?" Tony questioned, absent-mindedly twisting the length of Sally's neck cord around his hand. The captive woman sank to her knees, her fingers grasping at the lump thrusting against Tony's trousers. "I'll suck your cock for days, master. I'll suck it until I've sucked you dry, until my stomach's full-up with your come. I'll take your big cock up my tight bumhole and squeeze the come out of you. I'll do anything, master, but please don't put the whip across my arse."

Laura was desperate to play with herself, to finger her hard little clitoris; to be consumed by what she suspected would be the most shattering orgasm she'd ever reached. What the hell had been done to Sal? She'd always been a sniveller, sure, but what had happened to turn her into the miserable, shameless specimen huddled at her captor's feet, begging him to use her like a dog?

"How does your botty feel at the moment, slave?" Tony asked.

"Sore, sir—it feels sore."

"Tell me."

"My botty feels sore, sir, from the spankings you've given me."

"Did you deserve them, Sally?"

"Oh yes, sir, yes I deserved them. I'm a bad girl, master,

a naughty whore. I needed to have my botty spanked. I needed your big hard hand all over my botty, smacking it until it was red raw."

"What happens whenever you're disobedient, Sally?"

"I'm punished like a bad girl. I'm put across your knee, my knickers are taken down, and my arse is spanked, master."

"Your what?" Tony snapped at Sally and wrenched on the neck collar. An expression of panic flashed across the grovelling woman's face. "My botty, master," she stammered, correcting herself. "Tell me again—correctly this time."

"I'm put across your knee, my knickers are taken down, and my botty is spanked, master."

"What's your botty for, Sally?"

"It's for spanking hard, master."

Tony wrenched at the cord again, twisting Sally over and pressing his boot against her head, pinning it to the floor. Laura watched her friend's upturned buttocks tremble gently with the sudden movement and found herself staring at Sally's suddenly presented bum crack. Tony's arm flashed down, his hand dispensing rapid justice to the crimson cheeks.

"What is?" he growled. "What's for spanking?"

"My botty, master," Sally gurgled, wriggling her magnificent behind as Tony's hand landed on it time and again. "My botty's for spanking!"

"What else?" he growled, releasing her head from beneath his boot and swinging her around.

"It's for fucking, master, with your big hard cock."

"And…?"

Sally looked perplexed, her dark eyes searching her master's face for a clue as to what he wanted her to say.

"Do you want to feel the whip across your backside, slave-bitch?"

"No sir!"

"Then tell me what I want to know. What is it for?"

He slapped her hard across the face, and Laura felt a stab of pure excitement deep within her. There was something savage, cruel, about that kind of slap; something that reminded her of times when her ex had put his hand hard across her face, bruising her cheek and mouth; the same mouth that had later sucked so avidly on his dick as they'd made amends for their lovers' spat.

"It's for spanking and fucking, master, and…"

Sally was sobbing.

"Yes?"

"… and… and…"

Tony wrenched at the leash again, dragging Sally to her feet and once more twisting her around so that her bottom was facing the two seated spectators. He tugged again, causing her to stoop forward. His hand flashed down and slapped into her bumcheeks. The slaps were hard and vigorous, stinging the already-smarting red flesh.

"What's it for, Sally?" His palm continued to spank the wriggling cheeks in front of him.

"It's, it's for… for fingering, sir! Ow!!"

Smack, smack, smack.

"What's for fingering, you little bitch?"

Smack, smack, smack.

"Ow! Ah! My botty, sir! My botty's for fingering, sir!"

Smack, smack.

"And?"

"Oh, please, master! Please stop! My bum's so hot!"

"Your what, wench?!"

Smack, smack, smack, smack.

"My botty, master!"

"What's it for, Sally?"

Smack, smack, smack.

Sal needed to think of something fast, to try and stop the spanking hand. Much as she hated herself for it, Laura hoped her friend's next idea was a long time coming.

"It's, it's…"

Smack, smack, smack, smack.

"Ow! It's for shitting from, master!"

Smack, smack.

"My botty's for shitting from!"

Finally the rain of slaps stopped. Tony wrenched at the leash, forcing Sally to stand upright again. Laura squirmed about on the chair. Her eyes were focused on her friend's blazing scarlet buttocks. Her cunt, she knew, was wet with desire. Tony tugged Sally around. Her hot bare buttocks disappeared from view, replaced in Laura's eyeline by her friends' pair of jiggling titties. Sally's hands were on her cheeks, rubbing the sizzling flesh. She was breathing rapidly, a legacy of her wild and futile wrigglings while Tony had been slapping her bottom. He gently clasped Sally's wrists and guided her hands away from her buttocks.

Slowly, carefully, he moved behind her and lowered himself to his knees, so that her reddened flanks were at his eye level. His thumbs softly slipped between the burning cheeks and gently parted them. His face mashed against her scorched flesh, hot breath descending into the pit between her turgid cheeks. His tongue tickled against her back passage.

"Tell Kathy and Laura what I'm doing, Sally."

Her eyes focused on those of her seated friend. "He's licking my bumhole."

Suddenly, she swooned, and stumbled forward a little. Laura, who was convinced her sex had begun dripping its juices onto her chair, felt another stab of excitement at Sally's brief loss of balance. Tony inserted his tongue up her slave girl's ass.

"Yes!" Sally moaned, rising up onto her tiptoes and cupping her own breasts, clearly excited by the delightful feeling of her master's tongue making its way up her rectum. She leaned forward and clasped her own buttocks, wrenching them violently apart and pushing her bottom back into her master's face. She seemed desperate to impale herself proudly upon his tongue, desperate to feed as much of the burrowing intruder up her ass as possible.

Laura's mind was a whirl of confused thoughts. How could Sally be so eager, so keen, to be defiled and humiliated? Yet why was she herself so thoroughly wet, so desperate? And why didn't the scene being played out before her make her sick to her very core? She'd hated the feeling of a tongue up her own butt, and yet there was part of her, some element of her mind, that wished she was in Sally's position; costumed in rubber, beaten mercilessly on the ass, slapped cruelly across the face and ass-fucked with a stiff tongue.

"Oh master, I need something bigger up there! Something longer. I need your cock inside my tight bum! I want to feel you right up inside me!"

The master slipped his tongue from inside his slave girl's bottom. "No, Sally," he said, "I've got altogether different plans for you, my sweet."

"Please, master. Please stick your cock up me! Fill my bum with your big hard trunk, sir. Please, master. I need my botty fucked!"

Tony smiled, his hand stroking Sally's big, exposed left breast. "Maybe if you're a good girl, we'll put that right later. But for now, I have another little entertainment with which to amuse your friend here," Tony gently nodded his head in Laura's direction. "And I'm afraid I'm going to need your assistance again, Sally."

"What are you going to do with me, master?" A look of fear danced across Sally's face once more. "Oh, sir, please don't say you're going to beat my bottom again!"

"I'm going to treat you, Sally," said Tony, wrapping the excess length of leash around his hand and drawing his slave into him, "as you have never been treated before. I am going to introduce you, my sweet, to the exquisite delights of The Box."

At the clap of Tony's hands, two shuffling brutes clumsily made their way though the door. They were carrying between them what Laura could only imagine was the Box to which Tony had referred. They set it down on a nearby table and then shuffled across the room, taking up positions lurking in the shadows.

Laura stared at the Box. Made from wood, it was in the shape of a cube. Two opposite side panels had arch-shaped holes cut away, creating a tunnel of light within the contraption. Tony gripped one of the panels and lifted it clear of the object before doing the same with the opposite panel.

"Climb up on the table, Sally"," he instructed, "and rest on your elbows and knees against the floor of the Box."

"What are you going to do, master?"

"Did I say that you could ask questions?"

"No sir."

"Then you must be punished for doing so. Come here."

Sally dutifully approached her master, her head bowed in shame. "What do you think your punishment should be, slave girl?"

"You should put your cock up my bum, sir," Sally offered, a distinct enthusiasm in her voice.

"Your punishment, slave, not your pleasure."

She bowed her head again, and stared dolefully at her captor's boots. "I should be spanked, master."

181

"Where should you be spanked?"

"On my botty, master."

"Then present it."

Sally turned around and bent over, her bare bottom blooming out from within the tight rubber bondage suit. Tony wrapped his arm around the victim's waist—and then wrapped his hand around her large backside, slapping away at the already-scarlet flesh. Sally's naked cheeks began to wobble once again, and she squealed and wriggled wildly as her bottom was heated up. He applied twenty crisp slaps, making sure that every hot morsel of his slave girl's buttocks was left raw and smouldering.

Surely these impromptu spankings must have been sapping Sally of her strength, Laura thought to herself. She could only have been a couple of slaps short of complete numbness. No ceremony, no warning, no build-up, no growing sense of expectation—just the pain and humiliation of her bare bumcheeks being exposed and smacked.

Tony clutched her arms and pulled her up from her stooping position. "Tell me how your arse feels," he demanded.

"My arse feels hot and sore, master," Sally sobbed, "you've really spanked my naughty-girl bum. It's sizzling from the touch of your big hard hand, sir."

"Climb up onto the table, Sally, and crawl into the Box."

"Yes, master."

Laura watched Sally as she clambered onto the tabletop. Her eyes followed the movement of her friend's dimpled red bottom, framed by the black rubber bondage suit. She couldn't help but be titillated by the sight of Sal's curvy crimson buttocks, splitting apart and folding together as she lifted herself up onto the surface, crawled across the table towards the Box and crouched low to enter the contraption.

The Box was small and narrow, so-much-so in fact that Sally was resting her elbows and knees against its floor left her feet, ankles and bottom jutting out to one side of the structure and her head and neck overhanging the other. Tony took hold of the front half-panel he'd detached and slotted it back into place.

Laura suddenly realised the purpose of the arches. When the panel was fitted back in position, the curved wood pressed down against the back of Sally's neck and acted in the same way as a set of stocks, effectively trapping her head outside the contraption.

Tony picked up the second detached panel, the hole in which was bigger, and refitted it. The wood pressed down on Sally's lower back and against the flesh just below her ribs and above her waist. The effect was to box Sally in, leaving her bottom, ankles and feet poking out of the hole. The low position of the hole through which her head was poking had the effect of arching her back inside the Box, making her bottom rise high in the air.

Tony turned towards Laura. "Look," he said, "see what your friend has been reduced to? A head, two feet and an arse." He grinned broadly, exposing a set of beautifully white teeth. He was an attractive man, Laura noted, a fact which made his obvious cruelty—strangely—all the more alluring. "The Box is somewhat small, don't you think? Can you imagine her lovely body twisted into itself inside that hot, sweaty compartment? The important thing, of course, is that her head and her bum are both nicely exposed."

Tony turned his attention to Sally, who seemed to be in considerable discomfort, "Why do you imagine I want those particular parts of your lovely anatomy exposed, Sally? Why do you think I might want your head, or to

183

be more accurate, your sweet little mouth, available to me?"

Sally gasped for breath. Her trapped body was struggling to express itself, making a futile attempt to find a little bit more space inside her wooden prison. "I think you might want me to suck on your cock, master," she drooled. She had become hopelessly submissive in the time since Laura had last seen her. However bad the Farm had been, the American doubted her friend had succumbed to such a level of self-degradation as a result of the crude and brutish beatings the overseers applied. No, it was obviously the work of a more subtle, creative artisan. A man like the mysterious Sinfinder General, perhaps?

"What would you do if I put my penis in your mouth?"

"I'd suck you off, master." She gasped again. Laura could see that she was twisting her body as best she could inside the wooden structure, seeking a comfort that she had no chance of finding, "I'd suck on your big dick until you came in my mouth and then I'd swallow it all down."

"What else would you do with your mouth, Sally?"

"I'd suck on your testicles, master. I'd take your big juicy balls into my mouth so that my cheeks were full, and suck and lick them with my tongue."

"What about your rear, Sally? Why should I want that exposed."

"To spank and whip it, sir. To thrash it hard."

Tony moved behind his victim and began inspecting her bottom. It was thrust outwards, the cheeks forced wide apart by her pronounced position. Laura watched as his fingers wandered over the raw flesh, following a trail down towards Sally's crotch. He slipped two fingers between her thighs, pressing into her heated sex. "Ooooh!" Sally groaned, as the fingers toyed with her yielding flesh. They teasingly flicked at her clitoris, made it stand to attention.

Tony cupped the bulbous mound of her love nest with his hand and mashed his palm against her wet sex lips, forcing them to peel open. He massaged the secret flesh, making Sally moan with pleasure.

"You've got a wet, hungry pussy, Sally. What do you want?"

"I want your cock, master."

"Where do you want it?"

"Inside me. Inside my pussy—deep inside. I want you to fuck me with your big strong cock until you come."

"You'd like that, would you? You'd like me to come?"

"Oh yes, master!" Sally positively purred the words. "I'd love you to come inside me. I'd love to have my master's hot come inside my wet cunt."

Tony suddenly removed his hand and walked round to the side of the table. Clutching hold of it, he pulled firmly. The tabletop separated right in front of Sally's face, causing a narrow channel to appear. Her captor took firm hold of the Box and slowly raised the back-end up. Sally's bottom and feet rose into the air as the wooden contraption was turned on its side, gravity forcing her shoulders up against the front edge of her prison. The Box rested across the newly created precipice. Sally's head hung down in the chasm between the two tables. Her feet and buttocks pointed upwards at the ceiling. Tony stooped over her and gently licked the sole of her foot, sliding his tongue from the backs of her toes to her heel. She wriggled her toes in response, as though trying to escape the sudden, intimate attention.

"Tell me, Sally," he said, "were you spanked as a child?"

"No, sir," came the response from somewhere near Tony's kneecaps. "My mother would hit me with a

185

slipper, but she'd just lay it on whatever part of me was nearest, usually my arm."

Tony moved away, disappearing from Sally's narrow field of vision. "The slipper is for little girls, Sally. There are times, I think, when you are very capable of behaving like a little girl. When you do, we'll have to find out what effect the slipper has on you, especially when it's applied to the proper place."

He returned to the same position as before, standing right in front of his captive, his knees virtually in Sally's face, a two-pronged strap clutched in his hand.

"But for now," he said, "I think we'll treat you like the bitch on heat that you are." His arm dropped to his side. Sally gasped when she saw the wicked-looking implement of torture he was holding.

"No! Please, master," she murmured nervously.

"But I wish to see what effect a strapping has on you," her tormentor said coldly.

"Please no, sir. Don't strap me! If you have to punish me, please beat me with your hand!"

He ignored her plea. "It's the strap for you, my girl," he said, laying the length of leather along Sally's naked left buttock, "the strap across these naughty, wobbling hillocks. I'm going to teach you to respect the kiss of the tawse."

Tony raised the implement, bringing it down sharply against its intended target. The slap of the leather against flesh resonated around the room. From her seated position, Laura watched her friend's buttock tremble. Sally moaned, clenching her teeth and screwing up her face, battling to suppress her reaction to the stinging pain. The strap rested momentarily against her other buttock. Then it was removed, and swiftly returned to the fleshy surface of her upturned bum with a sickening splat.

Now Tony ran the strap along the peeled-open crease

separating her buttocks. The leather glided across the captive woman's sex lips and tickled her puckered anus. When she felt the strap being rested along the hairy groove, in just the same way as it had been lain on her buttocks, she flinched.

"No, master," she begged from the underside of the Box, "not there… please."

"You think these lovely holes should be left untouched, do you, Sally? All this soft pink flesh peeking out so naughtily from between your thighs should remain unpunished? And your tight little shit-hole—you don't think that should be slapped hard until it throbs. Is that what you think?"

He gently moved the leather back and forth, stroking the exposed flesh.

"Perhaps you'd better beg for mercy then."

Sally had no problem with that! "Please, master, please don't hit me there!"

"Where?"

"On my cunt and my bumhole."

"What should I do then?"

"Strap my buttocks, master. Strap them as hard as you want! Strap the skin off of them, but please don't strap my cunt!"

"What do you think I should do to this randy cunt?" her tormentor questioned, continuing to tease her sex with the strap, stroking the delicate flesh.

"I—I don't know, sir…" she stammered, seemingly at a loss to know what Tony wanted her to say. Her silence was her death knell. The strap was lifted and brought down, slapping against the flesh along the length of her clammy bottom cleft. The leather bit into the sensitive pink flesh.

"Then you must receive your punishment, you randy little minx!"

Again the strap hit home, causing Sally to scream out loud and beg for clemency. She tried to shift her flank away from the biting strokes, but she was unable to move it, even slightly. She was cramped and immobilised inside the Box, her bottom thrust upwards and out, exposed to the stinging discipline of the strap. One stroke followed another; the leather was unremitting in its attack on her soft pink flesh, lashing down a full ten times, tormenting her until she was squealing like an injured animal that was suffering an agony it could hardly comprehend.

Tony dropped the strap to the floor. Sally whimpered pathetically. Laura could see that her scalp and forehead were red from the blood rush to her head. Saliva dribbled from her mouth, giving her the look of a rabid, foaming madwoman. Laura tried to imagine how her friend must have felt, trapped inside the dreadful Box, her upper body squashed against her thighs, trembling and sweating inside the rubber bondage suit.

"Sally has certainly been a naughty girl," Tony smiled at Laura. "There's little question that her shameful behaviour was deserving of a thorough tawsing." His smile became a mischievous grin. "But we love her really, don't we?" He clasped her ankles. "So I'm going to show her just how much we love her. I'm going to make her lovely pink hole feel a lot better by giving it a thorough licking."

As Sally gasped in reaction to her master's declaration, Tony stretched her legs as far away from one another as the constraints of the Box would allow. He leaned over, lowering his head down between her parted ankles towards her bum-end. Musky scents from her soaking wet vagina rose into his nostrils.

Laura held her breath. She found herself trying to imagine the feel of Tony's tongue lapping against her own pink sex lips. Sally groaned at her master's touch as his tongue moved frantically, working her over—caressing her sex lips, tickling at her clitoris, occasionally slipping deep into her love channel. All the while, she groaned, and clenched and unclenched her toes—the only tangible signs of the mind-numbing pleasure her master was affording her.

At length, Tony lifted his head away from her fleshy sex and returned the Box to its previous position. He unfastened his trousers and pulled his thick erection from within. It was all Laura could manage to suppress a lustful moan.

Hands on Sally's swollen bottom cheeks, pulling them apart, Tony pressed his erect cock against her sopping wet vagina and pushed. She groaned as she was entered, the cock rubbing against her sore labia lips as it ploughed right into her slit.

Tony's cock sank deep inside her, pleasuring her soft wet flesh, threatening to burrow all the way into her womb. With a wicked smile in the direction of the two seated spectators, he rammed himself with extra force inside Sally. She squealed and clenched her teeth, screwing up her face as his cock churned up her insides.

Almost immediately, he gave a languid groan and began to tremble. Laura imagined Sally's vagina filling up with his spend, the hot fluid spurting deep within her hungrily sucking sex. For all the spanks, the slaps and humiliations, and in spite of the excruciating torment which being twisted inside the Box would undoubtedly cause, Laura found herself wishing to God it was her who was being pumped full of Tony's spend.

What the hell was happening to her as she sat there, dripping wet with desire and yearning for a cruel man to beat and fuck her? Sure, he was attractive—the first truly handsome man she'd encountered since her ordeal had begun—but what was it about him, about the situation, that was inexplicably turning her on?

Tony slipped from his captive mount, quickly fastening his zip and belt. Laura was consumed by another sudden, delicious thrill. A fast, vigorous fuck—lasting only as long as it had taken Tony to satisfy his needs—and Sally's pleasure had been brought to an abrupt end. He'd poked her and spent inside her, and then lost interest. There would be no tumultuous orgasm for Sal, no release from the tight, throbbing sensations of lustfulness she must undoubtedly have been feeling in her stomach and groin, just as Laura was.

Sally was a sex object, to be whipped and taken; to be used however her master desired. She meant nothing to him, concealed away from view inside the Box. Her head was free, so that she could pleasure his cock with her mouth; her arse was exposed so that her buttocks could be thrashed, her cunt and bumhole entered. The rest of her body was surplus to requirements, hidden away like the waste of flesh it was. The only things of value about her were the three deep holes she provided, and the access they guaranteed to the insides of her body; to her throat, her womb and her bowels.

Laura wished she could touch herself, yearned to bring herself off, to revel in the heady sensations of a body-wracking orgasm. Instead, she was forced to sit still and listen obediently as the naked woman beside her explained what the immediate future held.

"You will see your friend Sally again shortly, and perhaps another of your acquaintance," said Kathy. "In the meantime, you will accompany me to my bed chamber."

She snapped her fingers and ushered over one of the bulky brutes lurking in the corner of the room.

"Mute, you shall come too; we may have need of a big strong man."

190

The naked redhead smiled serenely at Laura, and for a moment, just a moment, she felt a strange empathy with her; a feeling that, in different circumstances, they perhaps could have forged some kind of friendship. As things were, the woman was about to lead her up to her bedchamber, and no doubt make some terrible use of her there. Strange. As they wandered from the room, Laura felt suddenly cold. The bizarre, burning passions inspired within her by the sight of a beautiful man torturing and pleasuring her best friend had suddenly subsided. Instead, there was a powerful sense of her own grim reality; a trip up the winding staircase with a round-bottomed redhead and a grunting brute, to endure whatever horrors they wished to perpetrate upon her cold and trembling body.

The redhead's bedchamber was vast. The attic of the house, the room had slanted ceilings with two horizontal oak beams running from one side of the roof to the other. Sprawling against the far wall was an enormous, four-poster bed, while an array of tables and cabinets offered homes for a variety of implements; objects and paraphernalia that Laura really didn't wish to know too much about. In the centre of the room there stood a four-legged wooden vaulting horse, complete with padded seat. Each leg was fitted with an iron manacle, and it was clear to Laura that Kathy used the object for reasons other than exercise—or perhaps more accurately, for the purpose of exercising her right arm only. Comfortable chairs and accompanying footrests filled the spaces in the two nearest corners of the room.

"Welcome to my parlour, little girl," Kathy teased, a wave of her arm encouraging Laura to cast her eyes over the contents of the attic chamber. "What fun we shall have in here. I have a great deal in store for you tonight, Laura my dear, so I suggest we begin. Mute," she turned her attention towards the shambling hulk who loomed behind Laura, "I don't think there's any reason for you to still be wearing clothes, is there? Take them off immediately."

Mute stripped naked, standing proudly to attention before the Sinfinder's right-hand woman, his cock magnificent in its hardness.

"Bring Laura over here please."

Mute took hold of the leash that still hung from Laura's neck and tugged her to where he had been directed. Laura watched as Kathy strode across to a nearby table and picked up a length of thick rope. She handed it to Mute and gestured to the wooden beam immediately above Laura's head.

"Throw the rope over there," she instructed. The naked brute did so, his huge cock swinging from side to side as he launched the rope upwards. "Fetch those." She pointed to a desk nestling in the furthest corner of the attic, underneath which two wooden-backed chairs were positioned, one stacked on top of the other. He placed them in front of her and awaited further instruction.

He was told to lift Laura onto one of the chairs and to clamber onto the other himself. He did as he was bade, acting immediately on Kathy's following order to fasten both ends of the dangling rope to Laura's wrists.

"Now get down and remove the chairs."

Laura felt the support disappear from beneath her feet. Her weight was taken by Mute as the chair slid from under her. He gently lowered her until the rope, fastened to her wrists and looped around the beam, was stretched and taut and she was left swaying gently from side to side in mid-air. The beam above her creaked ominously.

"Excellent," commented Kathy. She stood next to Laura's dangling body, her face level with the bound woman's hairy minge. Her hands slid up the sides of

Laura's legs, and came to a halt when they reached her waist. Fingers crawled onto her sore buttocks. "You've certainly got a lovely pair of breasts," Kathy whispered, a sly smile edging its way across her face, agitating her usually sullen jowls, "now let's have a look at your other delights."

Fingers crawled between Laura's buttocks and prised her dangling legs apart. One hand remained between her thighs, fingers fondling the flesh of her sex, a palm cupped the underside of her warm buttocks.

Now Kathy clasped a tuft of Laura's pubic hair and tugged upwards. The flesh at her groin was lifted, bringing into view the fat hood of her clitoris and the soft pink flesh of her cunt. The fingers resting between Laura's legs began to forage, padding against the folds of soft wet flesh, seeking a way inside her. Eventually, they found the opening for which they were searching. Laura tried to disengage herself from the exploring fingers, but Kathy held her in place with a warning tug at her minge.

"Soaking wet!" she exclaimed. She thrust her finger deep into Laura's love channel. "Drenched, in fact; like a girl who's feeling hot and lusty, and needs the feel of a tongue tickling away, deep inside her." Her smile broadened. "Well let me see what I can do for you."

"Screw you!" spat Laura, suddenly swinging her dangling body away from Kathy. Hot and horny she may have been as she'd watched Sally humiliated and used, but she would never, never accept the dreadful, sickening notion of being muffed by another woman!

Her flailing legs made her captor stagger momentarily, but the woman's firm grip on both her thatch of pubic hair and her scolded buttocks ensured that, ultimately, it was Laura who was the loser. Kathy's eyes flared angrily, the almost permanent scowl chiselled into her features seemed actually to darken. In two steps she was behind her captive, her hands again at Laura's buttocks. She tugged at the fleshy cheeks, forcing them open in spite of the American's best attempts to tighten her muscles and keep her bum-cleft sealed.

Laura winced as a sharp fingernail stabbed at her anus. With her left palm pressed against Laura's abdomen to steady her and ensure she didn't sway, Kathy pressed her finger against her captive's bumhole, twisting it backwards and forwards like a corkscrew, seeking a way beyond the tightly clenched ring of clammy, rubbery muscle. Laura tightened her sphincter, determined to keep the violator at bay, determined that nothing would enter her there.

She hated Kathy, hated the nonchalant, easy manner in which she went about the task of domination. She groaned as the finger worked its way past her clammy ass-muscle, the tip wiggling against the malleable inner walls of her anus. She squealed as the whole finger followed, pushing into her bottom-hole until it was fully inserted.

"Oh Jesus, no!" she ejaculated, as Kathy began to twist her finger first one way and then the other, prodding and poking at the spongy rectum walls, tickling Laura's tripes. Kathy moved her finger in and out, gently fucking the American's bottom. "You made a bad mistake just then, Laura," she said at length. "You were disrespectful and rude, and now, because of that, you are having your bottom finger-fucked. Perhaps you'd like to apologise to me."

Laura gritted her teeth and closed her eyes tightly. The finger was deep inside her, curling round to follow the curving contour of her back passage. The sharp nail scraped against the flesh of her rectum as Kathy's finger searched for the warmth of her bowel.

"I said, perhaps you'd like to apologise. Or are you are ready to receive a second finger up your arse?"

"No! No I'm not!"

"Then you'd better apologise."

A stony silence followed the suggestion, punctuated by the intermittent creaking of the wooden beam as it strained to support Laura's weight. She felt a second fingertip rest against the stretched flesh around her anus. The very real threat of a further assault was enough to draw a reluctant, stammered apology from her.

"That's better," said Kathy, sliding her finger from the clammy bum-pit, "It must be awfully embarrassing having somebody's finger up your arse, Laura. Isn't that the case?"

Laura exhaled and tried to control the involuntary twitching of her buttocks. She felt Kathy's fingers grip her cheeks and peel them apart again. Something wet smeared her anus. The second time it happened, Laura identified it as being the mistress's tongue, licking at her bum crack. She twisted her body; a desperate reflex action. Kathy let her do so. She could afford to; her hands—clamped against spanked buttock flesh—were holding her captive's bottom in position. In spite of her best struggles, Laura's anus remained exposed and vulnerable to the lashing tongue.

"Isn't that the case?" Kathy asked again between teasing licks. "Isn't it humiliating to have my finger up your arse?"

"Yes," Laura replied, hoping that muttering a response would stop Kathy from licking her bum.

"Then tell me, Laura, tell me it's humiliating."

"It is," the American offered, her legs still twisting and turning, trying to somehow effect an escape from the attentions of the ass-licking mistress, "it's humiliating."

"You'll have to do better than that," Kathy advised. She firmly poked the hard muscle of her tongue at the rubbery bottom-ring.

"It's humiliating to have your... your finger up my arse."

"Good girl. And how about my tongue? What's it like to have my tongue licking your arse-end, eating out your shameful bumhole?"

Laura knew what she needed to say. "It's humiliating," she mumbled, "it's humiliating to have your tongue licking my ass."

Kathy pulled her face away from the swollen red buttocks and Laura breathed a sigh of relief.

"You're a fast learner when you want to be, aren't you?" Kathy said. "If you continue to make such excellent progress, there really shouldn't be too much of a problem. Now. I want you to answer me honestly next time." Kathy walked around the dangling figure and looked Laura straight in the eyes. "If I were to let you down, would you offer me your lovely cunt to eat out?"

Laura visibly juddered, her eyes reflecting the mounting terror she felt at finding herself immobilised and at the mercy of the grim-faced redhead. She gulped hard, and found her throat to be completely dry.

"No!"

She was reproaching herself for giving such a foolish response even as she uttered the word. But there was really no point offering any other answer. She wasn't going to lie back and have her intimacies sucked, nibbled and licked by another woman, so what was the purpose of pretending otherwise?

"That's extremely unfortunate, Laura," Kathy said, "Because it means that instead of pleasure, I must give you pain." Her eyes flitted towards Mute, standing pathetically to the side of the room. "Come here, you big muscled brute," she said calmly, and watched as the man-beast shuffled across the room. Her hand clasped hold of his cock, which stood erect from his groin, huge and magnificent.

"What's this?" asked Kathy.

"My cock, mistress," the brawny, naked man replied.

"What would you like to do with it, Mute?"

"I'd like to fuck your beautiful cunt, Mistress."

"And?"

"And then I'd fuck your tight arse with it."

"Would you like me to suck you, Mute? Suck the juices from this shameless monster?" She squeezed his twitching muscle firmly in her hand.

"Yes, mistress! I would love that. Please suck my cock, mistress!"

"What, and run the risk of you emptying these great big balls into my mouth?" Kathy sounded horrified. "How dare you suggest such a thing! You are a shameful, puny man, Mute, and quite simply, you must be punished! I am going to spank this big cock and these swollen, naughty balls of yours until they are sore and shrivelled, and no longer pose a threat to me or to any other defenceless woman! Now get yourself over to the vaulting horse this instant!"

Kathy released the whimpering man, sending him on his way with a firm slap across the face. She turned to Laura. "I have no choice but to leave you hanging there, contemplating the punishment to come," she said. "This errant mongrel of a man must be disciplined immediately. You may well find that you enjoy watching him receive a sharp lesson in manners and good behaviour. Enjoy it as much as you can; I can assure you that you won't have much enjoyment when it's your turn to be disciplined."

She turned and paced purposefully across the room to Mute.

"Lie on top of the vaulting horse on your back," she ordered, and Mute immediately followed the instruction. The surface of the horse was narrow and curved, barely wide enough to support the man's muscular physique.

Mute's hands were fully employed clutching the sides of the padded seat along which he lay, desperately trying to ensure that he didn't overbalance and topple off. Unable to remove his hands even for a moment, there was no chance of protecting his genitals from the onslaught to come.

Kathy clasped his huge penis in her hand once again. "You are a shameful brute of a man," growled the flame-haired dominatrix, "who must be taught the only lesson you are likely to understand."

Her hand slapped the underside of Mute's huge, upright cock. "Bad boy!" she scolded. "I am going to spank this big nasty cock until it is hot and burning." Another slap, this time from the other side, "And don't for a moment think your swollen ball-bag will escape a thorough spanking either!"

She lifted his scrotum, forefinger and thumb encircling the bag at the join where it met the base of his cock, and, with her other hand, proceeded to slap away firmly at the swollen balls.

Mute wriggled and squirmed, his muscles flexing and unflexing as he struggled against the pain, struggled to retain his precarious balance on the vaulting horse.

"Perhaps when your genitals are nice and hot, you will remember you are in the presence of your master's assistant and refrain from making any more lewd and disgusting comments."

After applying a dozen sharp slaps to his testicles, Kathy returned her attention to spanking Mute's throbbing cock. Her smacks caused the big muscle to twitch excitedly and swing around, descending one moment towards his testicles, the next towards his stomach.

Laura noticed that the slaps were becoming less fierce. The Mistress's hand began to smack and then enfold the gigantic tool; smack and enfold, smack and enfold. Before long, the spanking had become a massage, Kathy clasping the erect organ in her fist and vigorously pumping the foreskin up and down.

"You're a naughty brute who's been punished for his bad behaviour," she announced, expertly wanking the enormous shaft, "and now this is to show you that you are forgiven. Bad brutes are spanked, good brutes are wanked."

Her hand increased the speed at which she was masturbating the massive cock. Mute's breathing became more erratic, more laboured. His muscles tensed, his fingers dug into the leathery padding of the vaulting horse. As his stomach began to rise and fall, Kathy leaned forward and engulfed his cock with her mouth. Within seconds he was groaning in ecstasy as his engorged penis pumped the contents of his testicles into the woman's throat.

Kathy withdrew the muscle, still caressing it with her hand, although more gently than before. There was no trace of come anywhere; she had obviously swallowed it all down, Laura mused as she dangled helplessly from the beam, aware that once again juices had been gathering between her thighs.

"Take Laura down," Kathy instructed her muscular foot soldier, suddenly releasing her hold on his penis and gently nudging him from his position on top of the horse. "Get her over this contraption with her bottom up and fully exposed. Let's see how she takes something a bit bigger than a finger up her arse."

"No!" Laura squealed, thrashing her legs around—as much as her irons would allow—in protest. Mute moved with admirable speed and efficiency. Before she knew it, Laura was being manhandled over the vaulting horse so that the blood rushed to her head. Her handcuffs were removed and each wrist was cuffed to a leg of the horse. To the other side of the padded seat, the irons were cast off and her ankles fastened to the contraption's two remaining legs. In this position, her stomach, abdomen and groin were all in contact with the padded seat, her bottom high and vulnerable.

"What are you going to do?" she whimpered. Her resolve was rapidly melting away with the knowledge that her most secret of places was about to be violated. Lips pressed against her anus. The lack of hands resting on her buttocks confirmed to Laura that her position— with her legs fastened wide apart—was so revealing that there was no need to separate her cheeks to gain access to her bumcrack. The tight little opening was already exposed. The lips planted a succulent kiss on the shameful hole.

"I am going to truly, comprehensively and thoroughly —" Kathy paused for effect "—fuck your arse."

Laura felt her stomach churn. Her nude body immobilised, her bottom exhibited, her wrinkled anus exposed to whatever fiendish tortures her captor wished to execute upon it, were not new experiences. Nor, after the spankings she had received from first Gerda and then Stephanie, was the ordeal of being spanked by another woman. But to find herself so cruelly exposed for the purpose of being used sexually by another woman, that was almost too much to endure. Her thoughts flitted back to the dormitory, to the night her holes had been eaten out by Lucinda. Even that had not seemed so mortifying, so shameful, as this; at least then Lucinda had been made to do it. And even though the blond had risen to the task with too much relish for Laura's liking, there had still been the fact that she'd been performing under command, under threat of being beaten herself.

Laura thought she was going to be sick.

And then she was suddenly distracted from the feeling of bile rising into her throat by an altogether different feeling—that of cold cream being dabbed against her sensitive bottom-mouth. It was followed by the uncomfortable sensation of an oily finger gliding up her tight, clammy bum-crack, tickling her bowels and thoroughly lubricating the soft flesh of her back passage…

Kathy was standing right behind Laura, pulling on a rubber glove. "Bad girls," she stated calmly, "are fucked hard in their bottoms. By the time I've finished with you, my lovely little whore, your bumhole will be so big you could put a tree trunk up there."

Laura twisted against her bonds, truly fearful of what her captor was intending to do. She didn't have to wait long to find out. Hands rested against her bottom and for a few moments, Laura felt her buttocks being mauled, twisted and squeezed; pulled wide until it felt as though the flesh was about to split, and then squashed together so that the inner folds of flesh were mashed into one another.

The removal of one hand was followed by the feeling of a 2 gloved fingers against her anus, and Laura knew that the assault was about to begin.

"You are a shameful, wilful girl, Laura," said Kathy as her fingers glided easily up the exposed anus, "I am glad I oiled you." The slimy lubricant ensured that their journey into the sanctum of Laura's bum channel was easily achieved.

"That's it," said Kathy, a third finger nuzzling at the wet bottom mouth, "wriggle around all you like, you wanton whore! It'll do you no good. You are bound and completely helpless, my fingers right up inside your bottom, feeling you."

"Please," Laura murmured, saliva dripping from her mouth as she clenched her teeth against the pain caused by the third finger's entry. "Stop it! I'll...I'll be good, I promise."

"If only you'd been good earlier..." A fourth finger, and a thumb, edged together past the cruelly expanded muscle of Laura's anal opening, forcing their way through the slime to join the other bowel-tickling digits. "None of this need be happening to you if you had been sensible in time."

"No! Uuhhh!"

Laura began to buck as she felt Kathy's whole hand twist and turn like a corkscrew past her ring of arse muscle, gaining access to her rectum, gaining entrance to the very core of her body.

"Yes, Laura! A thorough fisting should make you think twice about disobeying me again. You are lucky indeed that I don't tell the Sinfinder himself about your behaviour. He would introduce you to miseries of which you cannot even conceive."

Laura's eyes dripped with tears as she lay across the vaulting horse, her spanked buttocks upturned, Kathy's hand up her aching anus. The redhead began to gently move her arm backwards and forwards, nudging her fist deep into her captive's bowels, and then drawing it back along the clammy rectum. Sharp fingernails scratched at the yielding inner walls of flesh. Just when Laura thought the hand would pop out, releasing her bottom from the unnatural torment, it would instead plough forward again, back into her bowel, plugging her and making her gurgle and groan.

"I hope that you are learning from this dreadful humiliation, Laura. I hope you are learning that you must behave, that you must obey—just like your beautifully acquiescent friend."

Kathy continued to gently fuck Laura's bottom as she spoke.

"If you're sensible, you'll realise that obeying is by far the wisest course of action. Defy your masters, and your bottom will be punished, just as is happening now. Do not test me, Laura. I have no qualms about putting my hand up this tight arsehole of yours. I love nothing more, in fact, than to fondle a bound and naked woman's bowels; to watch her struggle for freedom while all the time I am exploring her shameful bumcrack; moving my hand in and out of her tight little arse until she pleads with me to stop, until she begs me to let her stool and stool and stool until her bottom is completely empty... do you want to stool now, Laura?"

"Yes, yes!"

"You don't, you know, it just feels as though you do. A nice juicy bum fuck always has that effect, no matter what you're being taken with."

Kathy removed her hand, and Laura felt a cold draft of air tickle her bum tunnel; evidence of the extent to which her tight anus had been cruelly expanded.

"Let me prove the point to you. Mute, bring me that nice, bristly bath brush."

"No, please! No more!"

"Do you wish you'd allowed me to eat out your lovely cunny, now, Laura?" Kathy questioned, peeling off the rubber glove, "Do you wish you had learned proper obedience?"

"Yes," Laura whimpered, her whole body heaving for breath as she struggled to recover from the traumatic anal assault.

"Perhaps you're not sufficiently regretful yet. Let's see if this helps." Kathy took hold of the bath brush and opened up her captive's bottom cleft again. Laura felt its cold touch against her bumhole. A gently exerted pressure encouraged the implement past the already-relaxed ring of wet anus muscle. She squealed as the bristles tickled her rectum flesh, and winced as Kathy turned the brush through a revolution, causing the bristles to scratch against her insides.

"Stop, please! Take it out! Don't fuck me with that!"

"Bad girls get their bottoms buggered with a nice bristly brush," Kathy informed her. "Jiggle those lovely moons as much as you like, Laura; this brush is going all the way up inside your arse-crack. I'm going to tickle your tripes for you, my girl, just see if I don't!"

The brush was nudged in and out, the bristles stinging Laura's anal passage. When it was removed after a few minutes, her bottom-crack stung and smarted almost as badly as her buttocks.

"Who is your mistress, Laura?" The question was greeted by nothing more than the sound of the bound woman's heavy breathing. Laura felt a slap against her right buttock. "I shan't ask you again," Kathy warned. There was nothing Laura could do. She had no means of escape, no way to protect her bottom from further treatment other than to acquiesce with Kathy's desires.

"You are," she whispered. "You are."

"Good girl! I can see that we're making real progress here. It hopefully won't be too long before I can actually believe what you are saying, and then all this unpleasantness can stop." Kathy snapped her fingers. "Bring me the dildo, Mute," she said.

Laura renewed her efforts to break free, twisting and writhing against the cuffs that shackled her to the horse.

Her abdomen slapped against the padded leather seat time and again as she fought to conceal her anus, to somehow remove her bottom from its vulnerable, thrusting position. Her buttocks jiggled wildly with the effort. All the while, even as she struggled, Laura was aware that there would be nothing more tantalising for her captor than the sight of her bare, spanked ass cheeks wobbling and shaking like delicious jellies.

She hated the thought that she was inadvertently exciting the stern dominatrix with her frantic buttock display, but what else could she do? How could she just lie there and allow a dildo to be thrust up her ass? In truth, given her predicament, how could she not?

"Thank you," Kathy said, and Laura surmised that Mute had handed her the dildo. "You might like this, Laura; you never know. Have you ever had need of a dildo before?" A stinging slap to her left buttock reminded her it was prudent at all times to answer quickly.

"No."

"Have you ever made love to another woman?"

"I'm not a lesbian."

"You might like it."

"I wouldn't!"

"You might. Let's see."

For the first time since her padded horse ordeal had begun, Laura was given the chance to look at another person. Kathy had wandered around the contraption and was standing by her side. Laura turned her head, her gaze wandering up from the woman's bare feet, calves and knees to her thighs, and then to her groin. It was hard for Laura to know how to react to what she saw. She was shocked; intrigued; uncomfortable; scared.

Kathy stood with her hands on her hips and her breasts thrust forward. Strapped around her waist was the enormous, grotesque dildo. Shaped like a male sex organ, its contours had been exaggerated—presumably to enhance sensation when thrusting in and out of a cunt or bumhole—it was hideously gnarled and twisted, its end fearfully bulbous.

"The Sinfinder had this made for me," she said. "He told me that I must use a nice big dildo to teach bad girls a lesson. And that's precisely what I intend to do."

With that Kathy disappeared from view again. Almost immediately, Laura felt her captor's hands rest against her buttocks, fingernails digging into the flesh as her cheeks were unceremoniously spread. The American clenched her teeth once more, flexing the muscles in her upper body, tightening everything—including, she hoped against hope, her well-ravaged anus.

"Please," she whimpered, her mind awash with images of the dildo, vast and unforgiving, being readied to plunge into the dark and clammy sanctum of her bowels. "Oh, please!"

"It's too late to plead, you wilful child," Kathy informed her. "I'm going to fuck your bottom with my great big dildo. Let's see how you squeal with a big fat plug up your shameful arse!"

It was the dildo Laura feared most. Kathy's hand up her bottom had been a surprise—she hadn't even known it was possible to fit a hand inside an anus—and the bath brush had seemed an impossibility, although the smarting flesh inside her arse-crack bore testimony to the mistress's skill in making the impossible come true. But the dildo; that was another matter entirely. It was sexual; it was strapped to another woman; it was about to be plunged into her bottom and she would be fucked hard with it.

Kathy's hand had investigated, explored; the bath brush had been used to torture, twisted to cause excruciating pain; but neither had actually fucked her, not really. The dildo was shaped like a cock and would be used like a cock. Kathy would rest her hands against Laura's thighs, and would thrust the contraption in and out of her bottom, buggering her.

"Prepare for a thorough bottom-fucking," the redhead warned. Laura felt the tip of the dildo against her throbbing anus. "Squeal like a pig, girly," her captor continued, "I'm going to bugger your arse with my nice big cock and make you howl! A well-fucked bumhole should make you realise once and for all that you must obey."

The tip of the massive tool nudged its way inside Laura's anus. She couldn't tell whether the huge weapon had been lubricated; it was entirely possible that no lube were needed, so pliable was her butthole after its previous ravagings. She felt Kathy press her palms firmly into her buttocks, guiding the cheeks even further apart, making her anal bud open even more. Then she felt the intruder move further into her arse-crack, ploughing forward against the tenderised rectum flesh, forcing its way into the dark cavity of her bottom.

"A... thorough... bum-fucking," spat Kathy from between clenched teeth. Her words were punctuated by her rapid, excited breathing. "A cock up your shameful hole, that should teach you!" Laura suspected she was right. There was no doubting the fact that she feared Kathy now; that however much she hated the red-haired dominatrix, she respected her as well—realised that there was nothing she could do to fight the woman's will, the power entrusted to her by the Sinfinder.

And how she could feel her power! She could feel it within her, plunging into her bowels. The massive contraption plugged her, and somewhere deep inside, in spite of herself, Laura sensed an inexplicable thrill—a delight almost—at the bizarre sensation. When the dildo was retracted, retracing its path along her bum tunnel until only its tip remained within her, she almost felt a sense of loss, but thrilled as well at the thought that the big fake cock would soon be plunged back into her.

And it was; time and time again.

Now Laura was really being used. The hands at her buttocks, holding them wide, kneaded the flesh. Kathy's thighs slapped against red cheeks as she forced her, filling and emptying her as the tool thrust in and out, sodomising her butthole.

"Bad girls get a stiff cock up their arses," Kathy growled, palm slapping down against hot bottom flesh. "They get their bums well fucked. You're getting your bum crack well fucked, aren't you, Laura? Tell me what's happening to your shameful arsehole."

"It's getting fucked," Laura wasted no time in answering, knowing that a pause would earn her a sharp slap on her already well-smacked buttocks.

"That's right, it's getting fucked; fucked with a big fat cock! It's a thrilling sight to watch this great big dildo disappearing up your arse. Do you enjoy the feeling, Laura? Do you like the feel of Kathy's cock up your bumhole!?"

"No."

"Why not?"

"It hurts."

"Are you ashamed, Laura? Do you feel humiliated; bent right over, stark naked and tied up, with a naked woman using a dildo to fuck you in the bottom?"

"Yeah. Yes I do."

"I'm all horny now!" Kathy accompanied her words with a series of long, powerful strokes, forcing the dildo even further inside Laura's anus. "I think I want a little satisfaction... Mute—put that lovely big cock of yours up my arse immediately."

She continued to thrust in and out of Laura's bottom, the dildo foraging relentlessly, churning the American's insides as it ploughed its course into her very gut.

"Do not displease me by causing me discomfort," Kathy instructed Mute. "Get your tongue into my arse and tickle my hole until it's wet and lubricated. I don't want to feel any pain when you stuff that great big monster of a cock into me! That's it! Right in! Move your tongue around; tickle the flesh inside my arse. Lick my bumcrack lovingly, you ugly brute. You are privileged indeed to have your tongue up your mistress's tight hole. Kiss and suck my ringpiece with care. Caress it—or I'll tell your master what you have done and he will have your hide branded with a white hot iron!"

The thrusts of the dildo were less powerful now. Laura could tell from Kathy's words that she was receiving a thorough tonguing from the shaggy brute. She couldn't help but imagine the scene; Mute kneeling behind the curvaceous, well-endowed female, his hands steadying her, pressed against her waist; his face pressed into her rotund, reddened buttocks, nose buried in the deep and clammy groove that cleaved her cheeks, tongue flicking and stabbing at her magnificently puckered anus.

"Eat my bumhole out, man-beast!" Kathy trembled as she spoke. Her movements caused the dildo to shift around inside Laura's bottom. "Get your tongue right up there and taste my arse! Ooh yes! Yes, that's it! Suck my tight arse-mouth!" Her hands squeezed Laura's buttock flesh, making the American wince in pain; fingernails threatened to tear the skin open.

"Now, brute!" Laura heard her growl. "Now! Put your dick deep inside my bumcrack! Fuck me until you fill my arse up with your hot come!... Careful... That's the way! That's it! You're all the way in now. Do it, brute!

Fuck my arsehole—hard!"

Laura squealed as the dildo bunged her rectum. Mute's powerful thrust into his mistress's anus forced the woman forward. Her thighs slapped against Laura's buttocks and plunged the dildo deep into her back passage. As Mute withdrew, so the dildo slid back along her bum channel. Mute thrust a second time, the full length of his cock again burying itself in Kathy's anus.

Again the dildo plunged into Laura's bottom.

"Ooooh yes! Fuck my big arse, you big brute! Fuck my fat bottom until you spend! Fill my rear right up with all that lovely cream. That's it! That's the way! Fuck my bumcrack, man-beast! Flood my big arse with your hot spend!"

The strange double bottom-fucking continued. As Mute's weight rested against Kathy, her body was mashed against Laura. Thighs slapped against buttocks, rigid implements fucked tight bottom-holes, Laura groaned and Kathy spurred Mute on.

"Take my breasts in your hands, beast! Twist my titties, maul the flesh. Yes! Keep that big stiff cock of yours thrusting inside my bumhole… Ahhh! It feels like my bum is going to be split in two, you big bad brute! Shame on you! Fucking your mistress's shit-hole with that stern, fat cock of yours!"

Kathy was gasping for breath. She was sheathed in sweat, her groin soaking Laura's buttocks as it slapped against them. Her fingernails tore at the American's skin as she urged her mount onwards.

"Fuck my fat bum as if I'm not your mistress at all, brute! Fuck me as if I'm a bad girl who needs her arse filled with hot come to teach her to behave!"

Laura had almost forgotten the discomfort she was feeling, so intrigued was she by the rapid change in Kathy's demeanour. The dildo had been ploughing relentlessly in and out of her rectum for so long that her anus was virtually numb. It almost seemed as though she had known nothing else, as though she had spent her entire life bent double and strapped up, a thick contraption remorselessly shifting inside her bottom, churning her up, plugging her to her very core. She could live with it now; live with the feeling of another woman's wet, naked thighs smacking against her buttocks; live with the feeling of the anal intruder fucking her bowels.

She could even handle the images inside her head, in which she was viewing the scene as a third person, and could see herself strapped to the horse—red, spanked bottom exposed—Kathy plundering her anus with the monstrous, cock-shaped tool. So now she was able to concentrate her attentions elsewhere. She could hear Kathy panting and gurgling. She knew from the force with which the woman was being invaded time and again as Mute thrust with increasing vigour.

"Bad girls need their arses fucked with a big, stiff cock!" Kathy gasped. "I've been such a bad girl! Ask me what I've done, man-beast!"

"What have you done, Mistress?" Mute managed to choke the words out between grunts as he thrust himself into Kathy's bottom.

"I've been fucking another girl with my big thick dildo—acting like a shameful lesbian. Punish me, brute; punish me with that great big cock of yours to show me what happens to shameless lesbians! Fuck my naughty tight arsehole until you come inside me. Punish my bottom, make it pay! Make my ringpiece sore, you big hairy ape!"

Kathy's body slammed for a final time against Laura. The dildo was right inside the American now, its whole length bunging up her anus. Mute moaned as he came, and Laura could only imagine the sight of his throbbing cock as it pumped his hot spend into the clammy interiors of his mistress's bottom-mouth.

"Good beast!" she commended him. "Let's make sure we squeeze every drop of that lovely spend out of you, shall we." Laura could feel Kathy flexing her muscles behind her, and knew that she was clenching her bottom around Mute's cock, drawing its fluids deep into her anus. The mistress slowly withdrew the dildo from her, and Laura felt a sudden, strange sense of loss and emptiness. Her anus felt sore and enormous; its soft flesh throbbed and ached. She was aware only of her bottom—of her spanked cheeks, her sodomised asshole—and wondered what dreadful punishment would next befall her tender posteriors.

"Unfasten her, Mute."

The huge, heaving brute of a man did as he had been told, helping Laura to her feet. She staggered momentarily, unused to the freedom, and felt the pressure in her head gently subside. The panting Kathy took hold of the leash that was still fitted around Laura's neck.

"One more little display to see," she said, "and then you will be handed over to the Sinfinder's ministrations. I work only to ease the way for him, and perhaps now, after our little game, you will have the good sense to be obedient."

She gave a gentle tug on the leash, urging Laura to follow her, and left the attic bedchamber. They returned to the room where Laura had earlier watched the rubber-bondaged Sally endure—or was that now enjoy? —her dreadful humiliation. She was ordered to sit on the same chair from which she had viewed the earlier scene, and pressed her throbbing buttocks tentatively against the hard wooden seat.

Kathy sat next to her, retaining a hold on the leash. What now, Laura thought to herself. What new vision of depravity was she about to be made to watch? There was a noise from the other side of the far door, and she knew she was soon to find her answer.

15

At the far side of the room there was a length of fencing, fastened to the floor by bolts. Laura heard the sound of the door opening. Two figures emerged into the light, and when she recognised them, her heart skipped a beat. It was Sally again—once more required to perform, to humiliate herself, in front of her friend—and the haughty Lucinda—who Laura had last seen being cruelly beaten in one of the communal toilet cubicles back at the Farm.

The women were dressed in the style of cowgirls, except for the fact that they didn't carry guns. They sat down on the floor around a heap of twigs that had been arranged like firewood. Two bulky saddlebags were stacked behind them, near to the fence. The door through which the Mistress had led Laura slowly opened and a tall well-built young man entered the room. He was followed swiftly by a second male, shorter and darker— Laura was uncertain as to whether she'd seen them downstairs in the cellar.

Both the men were dressed in cowboy gear. Both were brandishing their revolvers. "Well what we got ourselves here?" said the taller man, affecting a mild western-American drawl. "Looks like we got ourselves a couple o' pretty missies!"

"Sure looks that way, Clancy," replied the second man, moving forward beyond his partner and circling around the seated figures. "Stand up, ladies, if you please. We got some business with the two o' you. Perhaps you'd care t' tell me 'n' my brother Ike, here, just exactly what yer doin' on our property."

It was Lucinda who replied, mumbling the words almost incoherently: "We didn't know it was your land. We're sorry if we've done anything wrong."

"You is trespassin', lady—trespassin' on Clanton

property. Ain't nobody does that 'n' gets away with it."

The dark man moved in close on the women.

"Now we is gonna teach you a lesson you ain't never gonna forget. Ladies, do me the favour of bending over that there rail, would you." Laura was certain that she heard Sally sniffle. The two cowgirls seemed to hesitate. It was hard for the American to tell whether they were simply playing the game as they'd been told to or were, in fact, still fearful of the dreadful treatments that had been so much a way of life for them all those past few days.

"I'd do as my brother says if I was you, ladies. Get your hides bent over that rail, 'n' quick about it!"

Sally and Lucinda turned around and leaned forward, side-by-side, over the length of bolted fencing.

"Let's see what these girls keep inside their britches."

The two men unfastened the women's trousers, unceremoniously wrenching them down as a testimony to their lustfulness. The women's shirts were flipped back, baring their bottoms. The taller man stooped down and picked up two twigs from the makeshift campfire, handing one to his companion.

"It is the judgement of this here court," he declared, "that these here ladies is trespassers and criminals,' n' as such, is to be punished like the pair of shameful whores they is!" He paused for effect and used his gloved fingers to tweak the corner of his bushy—probably stick-on, Laura surmised—moustache. "It is therefore our judgement that they is to be whipped on their bottoms with birch twigs and is then to be roundly fucked in their asses, 'til such time as their asses is full of Clanton seed."

He stood back and swung his birch twig experimentally through the air. The dark man followed suit. "Let the whippin' begin," he growled, and the birches flew through the air, landing simultaneously on the two

215

upturned bottoms. Sally and Lucinda howled, both lurching up from their bending posture and tossing their heads backwards.

The tall man clutched a morsel of the buttock flesh in front of him, "Get yourselves back over that there rail, ladies, 'fore I go 'n' get my hot iron and brand your asses with more than just a few birch marks! Get those heads down 'n' those asses up!"

The women did as they were told, reassuming their position just in time to feel the cut of the twigs again. Again they reared up like squealing horses having their flanks branded; again hands mauled their buttocks as they were guided back over the fence.

The birch twigs continued to strike soft bottom flesh, the women's hindquarters twisting and gyrating in a wild and feverish dance. Only by clutching the posts of the fence were Sally and Lucinda able to retain their punishment position, coughing and choking for breath as their bottoms were worked over by the twigs.

It was almost a relief when the tall man declared, "now you is gonna get fucked in youse asses."

The cowboys wrenched the cowgirls' trousers right down to their boots; each licked a thumb and inserted it in the women's bottom-holes. Moving in close behind them, they ripped open their own trousers and thrust their cocks up the puckered bum cracks, vigorously plunging in and out, burying their throbbing erections to the very hilt.

"Youse cowgirls is gonna get a real fuckin' in these tight little butts o' yourn. Those asses is gonna be so big and wide, youse gonna be shittin' into yo britches all day long!"

The cowboys laughed at the joke and thrust until they trembled in orgasm, ejaculating deep into the cowgirls' tripes. Pulling themselves free, they stuffed their cocks back into their trousers, and told the women they were free to get up and get dressed. Within moments, the troupe of performers had disappeared through the door, leaving Laura to wonder what terrible devilments had been inflicted on the two women to make them so seemingly acquiescent.

"A beautiful performance, I'm sure you'd agree, Laura," said the Mistress, gently tugging on the neck collar. Behind her, Laura could hear the door gently creaking open. "Do you see how well the Sinfinder has trained your two friends? They were not so temperamental, so strong-willed as you, and needed less time on the Farm. Because of that, they have already been prepared for their new lives, travelling the world with the Sinfinder's circus, performing such delightful shows as this to captivate the crowds."

The buxom redhead smiled serenely.

"That will be you soon, Laura. The Sinfinder has great plans for you, my sweet, great plans indeed." The Mistress craned her neck and looked towards the door. She nodded her head in gentle acknowledgment of the figure who was standing there. "She is ready now, master," she said.

Laura craned her neck too, and gazed upon the dark-costumed, satanic figure of the man she could only assume to be the Sinfinder General.

"Excellent," murmured Matthew Hopkirk. "Then we shall begin…"

The End